KID HAILER

Youngster Wayne Hill had finally found work, as a sheep herder with Rocking R boss Bill Lessman. Nominated for a mountain term with his own herd, he hadn't bargained for cattle boss Fox of the FX spread, who wanted the Government range back at any price. Soon Wayne found himself in a desperate showdown with a gunman and the cattleman . . .

BILLY HALL

KID HAILER

Complete and Unabridged

LINFORD
Leicester

First published in Great Britain in 1990 by
Robert Hale Limited
London

First Linford Edition
published March 1992
by arrangement with
Robert Hale Limited
London

British Library CIP Data

Hall, Billy
  Kid Hailer.—Large print ed.—
Linford western library
I. Title
823.914 [F]

ISBN 0–7089–7167–9

Published by
F. A. Thorpe (Publishing) Ltd.
Anstey, Leicestershire

Set by Words & Graphics Ltd.
Anstey, Leicestershire
Printed and bound in Great Britain by
T. J. Press (Padstow) Ltd., Padstow, Cornwall

1

"KID, if you're as young as you look you better go home."

The kid whirled, bristling, towards the speaker. The face he looked into was lined and wrinkled brown like a sun-dried piece of leather. Only the eyes were young that twinkled with amusement at the red blush that sped from his collar to his dark hair, combed straight back.

The kid snapped, "I'm old enough to do a man's work any day!"

The weathered rancher rolled a wooden match from one corner of his mouth to the other. He reached one index finger to his forehead and pushed his beat-up Stetson to the back of his head and looked the kid up and down. The kid stood barely five-nine, with legs almost comically short. His long torso was powerfully built, however. His

1

bulging shoulders and thick chest spoke
of immense power out of place beneath
the childish roundness of his face.

"You lookin' for work?"

"Uh huh."

"Know where you are?"

"Waltman, Wyoming, I guess."

"Why'd you come here?"

"Fella back home told me there was
usually a rancher or two here to meet
the train when they needed hands."

"Where you from?"

"Nebraska. Folks ranched over by
Marsland."

"Why'd you leave?"

"My dad died. Got pneumonia."
The kid swallowed hard. He looked
like he was about to stop, then plunged
ahead. "Ma's got three kids younger'n
me. My other brother he ain't much
good. Figured if I could get work up
here I could send a little money home
to help out. I know stock, and I sure
do work hard."

"Why didn't you get a job there?"

"Ain't much work around there.

2

What there is only pays about fifteen dollars a month. Can't help much on that. Heard you paid better up here."

The rancher thought about it, then nodded his head. "All right. Ever herd sheep?"

"Sheep!?" The kid took half a step back. "I came here to punch cows, not herd sheep."

"Up to you. I got sheep about to start lambin' and I need hands. I pay forty a month and your keep."

He waited while the kid thought about it. The kid asked. "What happens after lambin's done?"

The rancher took off his hat and ran his fingers through his reddish grey hair and looked off across the country. He looked back at the kid and studied him for several minutes, then put his hat back on.

"If you show me you can handle 'em I'll send you to the mountains with a band of sheep for the summer. I furnish your dogs, sheep wagon, ammunition, and grub. If you want half your wages sent to your ma every month, I'll send it for you. The rest of your wages you can collect whenever you go to town, but you can't be goin' to town when your sheep are on the mountains."

The kid was thinking fast. He'd never worked sheep, but he'd listened many times when others talked about it. He'd always dreamed of being a hand on one of the big Wyoming cow outfits, but dreams must wait behind the realities of survival. He shrugged his shoulders.

"I've never worked sheep, but if someone lines me out I guess I can handle it."

"All right, you're hired till I see how you do. If you don't work out I'll give you your walkin' papers quick though."

"Sounds fair enough."

"I'm fair. I treat my hands right, but they all pull their weight. You can throw your stuff in that Model 'T' out front and I'll be along in a few minutes."

He turned and started away, then stopped and faced back. "Oh, what's your name?"

"Wayne. Wayne Hill. Yours?"

"Bill Lessman. Outfit's the Rockin' R."

As Lessman walked away Wayne picked up his saddle, his bedroll, and his thirty-thirty carbine. He carried them through the depot and out the front door. Sitting in the dust at the street's edge was an open-topped automobile. He looked it over, then dumped his gear in the back. He walked around it twice, struck by its strangeness. He tested the door handle. When the door opened he got into the passenger seat and sat back to wait for Lessman.

"Well," he muttered to himself, "it's a job."

"There's another load over at the store you'd just as well help carry."

Lessman's voice startled him. He hadn't seen him come from the general store. He dumped a hundred-pound bag of flour from his shoulder into the back, then loaded a box of canned goods he had held under his other arm.

Red-faced, Wayne jumped from the car and accompanied him back to the store. As they entered he spotted the groceries stacked together. At the front of the stack were two hundred-pound bags of potatoes. He walked over to them, leaned forward and wrapped one arm around each of the bags. Straightening, he swung a bag of potatoes to each shoulder, turned sideways to get through the door, and walked easily across the street with them.

He heard the grocer behind him as he stepped into the street. "Can you still do that, Bill?"

"Ain't about to try, Walt. Ain't as young as I used to be. Whole lot more man than he looks, though, ain't he?"

"Well, he's sure stout anyway," the grocer agreed.

When they had re-arranged the load twice to get everything into the Model

6

'T' they headed north out of town. It seemed to Wayne that they were going much too fast for the road, but he kept from saying anything. He knew cars were different from the horses and wagons he knew, and figured Lessman must know what he was doing. He tried to keep from hanging on. It wouldn't do to let his new boss think he was afraid, even if he was.

The country he saw was a disappointment. He had expected mountains and timber. The mountains were there in the distance, both to the northeast and to the west. The air was sharp and clear, so he knew this country was high, but there wasn't a tree in sight.

Small clumps of salt sage were interspersed with larger varieties of sage brush that grew to six or eight feet high. The draws between the hills showed greasewood, with buck brush and wild rose bushes clustering in the heads of the draws. The backdrop of the mountains gave the country an open and free look that Wayne liked, even without timber.

The country grew steadily rougher. The road crossed ridges and twisted down across deep draws until Wayne lost track of how many they had crossed. At the bottom of one hill Lessman stopped the car and turned it around.

Wayne asked, "How come we're stopping?"

"Gotta back up the hill."

"Back up the hill? Why?"

"You ever ride a Model 'T' before?"

"No. Seen a couple, but never been in one."

Lessman nodded. "Thought so. Funny thing about a Model 'T'. It's got a lot more power in reverse than in low. If you can't pull a hill in low you gotta turn around and back up it."

"It won't pull this hill?"

"Not forwards. Oh, it might empty, with a good run, but we're loaded pretty heavy. You might have to push."

Wayne got out and followed as Lessman began up the hill. He had no trouble keeping up, and when he heard the motor start to lug down he took a grip on the front bumper and leaned into the grill, digging his boots into the dirt and pushing. He could hear the difference on the motor immediately when he started pushing, and they made it to the top of the hill.

When Lessman stopped he got back in, panting: "Boy, I'm out of breath! I didn't think I was pushing that hard."

Lessman shrugged. "You're just not used to the height. You're maybe three thousand feet higher'n you're used to. We'll be another fifteen hundred feet higher yet at the ranch. You'll get used to it."

"I didn't think there'd be that much difference."

"Yeah, there is, though. You'll find the sun's hotter here too. You'll likely burn some, come summer, even if you are used to being out all the time."

The road swung more easterly and the mountains were directly ahead. Wayne knew they were climbing all the time, and the sage brush began to be interspersed with scrub cedar trees. An occasional pine or isolated clump of aspen promised they were getting closer to timber country.

Wayne asked, "How far is the ranch?"

Lessman thought for a minute. "I suppose about twelve or thirteen miles from here. It's twenty-eight from Waltman. That's why I brought this here Model 'T'. I can make it in three or four hours in it. Takes an awful long day on horseback."

As they drove, Lessman's forehead creased into a deepening frown. Every few minutes he would reach up and scratch his head behind his right ear. The match he continually rolled from side to side in his mouth grew shorter and shorter as he chewed on it. Suddenly he jerked the match from his mouth and threw it angrily out of the car.

"Kid, I guess I owe it to you to tell you. We may be in for some trouble.

10

They's a gol-danged cow outfit up north pushin' for some of our range."

Wayne was puzzled. "How can they do that? Don't you own it?"

Lessman shook his head. "Naw, we don't own nothin' only the home place. All the range up on the mountains is government range."

Wayne still didn't understand. "What do you do, get permission from the government to use it?"

Lessman gave a short chuckle. "Boy, you are green, ain't you? Naw, we just use it. It's just always been first-come, first-serve. Everybody's pretty well got the range they use every year, and everybody else stays off of it. Only the last year or two one of the cow outfits has been tryin' to push us off of what we've always used."

"You mean like a range war?"

"Oh, I don't think it'll come to nothin' like that. They may leave us alone now, or maybe try to scare the herders off, or just make life miserable.

This ain't the wild west no more, you know."

Wayne was not reassured. Something in Lessman's voice lacked the conviction it ought to have. Wayne craned his head to be sure his thirty-thirty carbine still stood on the back floorboard where he had put it, directly behind his seat. He began to scan the country ahead on both sides of the road, alert for anything out of place, but having no idea what he was watching for.

The road topped out on a long hogback and followed a brushy ridge with frequent clumps of aspen. Directly ahead Wayne caught the glint of the westering sun reflecting from metal in a clump of trees. He pointed and shouted, "Look out! Someone's in those trees!"

Just as he shouted Lessman gave a sudden grunt and Wayne saw a round hole appear magically in the windshield. He was already moving when the report of the rifle reached him. He grabbed his thirty-thirty as he lunged over the car's side, and heard a 'thud' into the seat where he had been sitting an instant before. He hit the edge of the road with a jar and rolled into the brush.

Gathering his feet under him he plunged in a long dive into the brush, rolled to his feet and took seven or eight running steps toward the trees housing the rifleman. He stopped, panting breathlessly, crouched behind a clump of sage brush.

Bullets crashed into the brush where he had landed. The Model 'T' had continued about thirty yards, angling off the road, until it bumped up against a big clump of soap weed. There it lurched once and the motor killed.

Wayne fought to control his breathing and his temper. Strangely, he was not afraid. He was angry. "Yellow-bellied dry-gulcher," he muttered. "You picked the wrong victim this time."

He steadied his breathing and removed his hat. Laying it on the ground he stood in the centre of the clump of sage he was hiding in, rising far enough to look toward his attacker. He caught a glimpse of movement in a clump of aspen about a hundred and fifty yards away, just beside the road. He slowly raised his rifle to train on the spot and waited.

Time hung suspended while he waited. He had almost decided whoever was there had gone when a hat appeared. He watched the hat move out from behind a tree until the head beneath should have appeared, but didn't. "Try again," he gritted through his teeth. "I ain't dumb enough to fall for that."

The hat disappeared, then reappeared on a man's head leaning to peer around the tree. He held his fire, remembering his father's words: "Never try for a head shot if you have a choice. Go for the shirt, right between the pockets. It gives you more room for error. If you miss a little, you've still got him. If you miss a head shot you just plumb miss, and he gets the next shot."

He saw the man look around carefully, trying to determine whether he had hit the second man or he had left. Slowly he stepped from his cover and started toward the stalled car. As he stepped into the clear Wayne shouted, "Far enough! Drop the gun."

The man whipped toward his voice and jerked his rifle to his shoulder, firing at the sound of Wayne's voice. He heard the bullet tearing through the brush beside his head as he held his breath and squeezed the trigger of his own rifle.

Over the gun barrel he saw the puff of dirt from the man's shirt front and a look of stunned surprise cross his face. He looked toward Wayne's place of concealment with his jaw hanging wide and working spasmodically. Then his knees buckled and he fell to his knees, then forward onto his face and lay still.

Wayne stood without moving for several minutes. He supposed the bushwhacker was alone, and he was pretty sure he was dead, but he wasn't about to take chances. After several minutes he lowered himself into the brush and picked up his hat. He put it on the end of his rifle barrel, crouched a couple feet below it, and started walking toward the road. Nothing happened.

Putting his hat on, still crouched, he reversed his direction and worked quietly through the brush to the opposite side of the clump of aspen. Moving past the single horse tied in the edge of the trees he reassured himself there was no second gunman.

With his rifle ready he walked to the man he had shot. He saw where the bullet had emerged from his back, and knew he was dead. He hooked the toe of his boot under his chest and turned him over. The pinched face and the pencil-thin moustache looked crafty and deadly, even in death.

Wayne looked at him for a moment, then felt a sudden rising in his stomach. He whirled away and retched violently. His face white, his legs trembling, he looked back at the dead man.

Up to that point he had acted without thought of consequences. He had done the things his father had carefully trained him to do. Now, suddenly, he was faced with the stark reality that he had killed a man. He had coldly and without feeling put a bullet into a man's chest and watched him die.

His heart began to pound. He felt the increasing tempo of his heart pounding against his temples. He reached out to grab a tree, but it seemed to sway in a circle around him. His knees buckled and he sat down abruptly on the ground. Sweat sprang out on his face and his breath came in ragged gasps. He sat there, leaning against a tree for several minutes before his heart slowed and his head began to clear.

He lunged abruptly to his feet. "Lessman! I forgot Lessman! He's been shot, and I forgot him!"

He sprinted to the car and jerked the driver's door open to stare into the business end of a forty-five Colt.

Lessman was lying across the seat with his gun in his hand. When he saw it was Wayne he lowered the gun and spoke through ashen lips: "Boy I'm glad to see you, Kid! Is he gone?"

Wayne swallowed twice and licked his lips. He looked back toward the dead gunman, then back at Lessman. "Uh, he's uh, he's dead. I, I shot him. You OK?"

Lessman struggled to sit up. "I'll live. Guess you wouldn't know who it was. What'd he look like?"

Wayne's brow furrowed as he looked toward the dead man. "Small guy, maybe my height, but skinny. Wore a flat-crowned hat. Had one of those little thin moustaches. Had a forty-one Colt in a tied-down holster. I never saw anybody wear one of those."

Lessman suppressed a groan as he moved. "Don't sound like nobody I know. How'd you kill him?"

"I didn't want to kill him. I tried to get him to give up. When he shot I dived over in the brush a ways and waited. When he came out of the trees I hollered at him to drop his gun, but he wouldn't. He shot at me, so I shot him."

He helped Lessman struggle his shirt off. The bullet had taken him high in the chest, just under the collar bone. The bleeding had nearly stopped. Lessman said, "That's a lot better reaction than a kid oughta have. Where'd you learn that?"

"My dad taught me. Used to make me practise being ready for surprises. He always said it's how you react to the unexpected that kills you or keeps you alive."

"Well, that's hard to argue with when it's just kept us both alive. Think you can drive this thing?"

"No! I can drive anything you can hitch horses or mules to, but I ain't never been in one of these things before."

"Well, I guess you're about to learn. If I try to drive I'll keep this wound bleedin' all the way home. It's just got to be up to you. I'll tell you what to do. Get in and let's go."

"What about the guy I shot?"

"I'll send a couple of the hands back to bury him when we get home. Better get his guns and throw them in the car. Then get me home so's my wife can fix up this bullet hole."

Wayne returned to the gunman and stripped off his gunbelt. He picked up the rifle from the ground and put them both in the back, amongst the groceries. Lessman set the throttle while he climbed into the middle of the soap weed to crank it, then told him how to shift gears, advance the spark as he started, and how to pull the gas lever and clutch at the same time.

He put the car into gear and released the clutch too fast. The car made one big lunge and killed. As he got it started again Lessman moaned, "Hope you don't do that too many times."

Wayne tried again and jerked the car violently, but kept it running. He pointed it toward the road, but failed to get turned onto the road before he was out in the brush on the other side. Over-steering wildly he whipped back toward the road, then careened from edge to edge of the road until he began to get the knack of it. Sweat stood out on his forehead and his knuckles were white as he gripped the steering-wheel, but they wobbled generally up the road.

2

AS the road rounded a curve in the bottom of a wide valley they came in sight of the ranch. Wayne took stock of the lay-out and was pleased. The ranch house was built near a low red-rock cliff that formed the west wall of the valley, sheltering the yard from the worst of storms. The bunkhouse sat about fifty feet north of the house, backed against the same cliff. Three small houses formed a line past the bunkhouse, with the barn and corrals across the yard.

As they entered the yard Wayne began to squeeze the bulb of the car's horn. At its insistence a couple of hands came into the yard, then a woman appeared on the house porch, wiping her hands on her apron. As he wobbled the car to a sliding stop in a cloud of dust he yelled: "Mr Lessman's been shot! Somebody come and help him!"

He noticed with surprise that Lessman's wife wasted no time with squeals nor tears. She ran to the car and tore away the bandage, looking at the wound, then back at Lessman's face. Lessman was already trying to reassure her. "It's not bad," he gritted. "It didn't hit nothin' to amount to much, but it's gonna take some healin'. One of you boys might steady me some so's I can get into the house."

One of the men — obviously the foreman — said, "Pete, you and Morgan help him in the house. Curly, run over to my house and tell my wife Mrs. Lessman needs some help. Kid, you come here and tell me what happened."

Wayne didn't hear him. He was staring at the girl who had followed her mother to the porch at the sound of the car's horn. She was about sixteen or seventeen, he guessed, with a row of freckles across her cheeks and the bridge of her nose. Her hair was red, but not the orange red of most redheads. It was a deep auburn red, and was tied back from her face with a single green ribbon. Her brow was furrowed with concern, but like her mother she lost neither time nor energy with hysterics. She held the door open for the two men helping her father, then followed them into the house.

He stood there staring at the place she had been until the foreman said, "If you're done gapin' at the boss's daughter now, you can tell me what happened."

Wayne started, then turned red. "Oh, sorry. I was, uh, I was, uh, yeah. Guy in the trees shot at us. Man, I never drove one of them things before! He told me what to do. I think it bounced him around awful bad."

The foreman held up a hand. "Whoa. Whoa. Back up a ways. Who are you?"

"Wayne Hill. Folks just call me 'Kid'. Mr Lessman hired me in Waltman. I come in there on the train."

"OK. Now start at the beginning and tell me what happened."

Wayne started with the loading the groceries and the drive home and filled him in on the story. When he had finished the foreman nodded. "OK. My name's Curt Brewer. I'm foreman. You can take your stuff to the bunkhouse. You ever work sheep?"

Wayne took a deep breath. "Nope. Worked cattle and horses. Never been around sheep."

Brewer smiled a little. "Neither did we till five years ago. Cattle market got so bad the boss decided it was switch to sheep or go broke."

"They hard to handle?"

"Naw, they ain't half bad to work with after you get used to 'em."

He turned to one of the other men. "Scotty, you come with me and we'll drive this thing back and bury that guy the kid says he killed and do somethin' with his horse. Sounds like maybe that hog-back above Dry Crick."

25

The hands had already unloaded the groceries from the car and he removed his gear while Scotty cranked it back to life. As they wheeled from the yard he picked up his saddle and carried it into the barn. He swung it across the rail where the others were kept and looked around. It was a solid, well-built barn with twenty stalls for horses. Two of the stalls had been equipped with stanchions for milk cows.

"They got milk cows!" he marvelled. "Some of the hands must have kids. Wonder if we get milk with meals."

He turned back to the yard, picked up his bedroll and rifle, and went to the bunkhouse. He stopped just inside the door to let his eyes adjust to the darker interior, and looked around. Walking by the large wood stove he picked an empty bunk and unrolled his bedroll onto it. He took his extra clothes and other odds and ends that were rolled into it and put them in a drawer under the bunk.

He hesitated a while before he put

one item into the drawer. It was New Service Colt forty-five in a worn holster. It was not a fast-draw holster, nor a long enough cartridge belt to allow for the low-slung, tied-down arrangement he had noted on the man he had killed. It was, simply, a cowpoke's working sidearm. All cowboys on the range carried one. It could save his life from an angry cow or an unexpected rattle-snake. Placing it in the drawer he heard the door open and close behind him. Turning he saw the first thing on this ranch he didn't like.

"Howdy!" the newcomer offered.

He had stopped just inside the door as he and Wayne looked each other over. He was probably mid-forties, wore a week's stubble on his face, and the sleeves of his shirt were rolled up, but his long underwear was not. The arms of his underwear were black and slick with grime.

"You're the new kid, huh?" As he asked he scratched his stomach that dropped over the belt on his frayed and filthy levis.

"Uh huh. Just got here."

The man shifted a chaw of tobacco from one cheek to the other. A trickle of tobacco juice followed down the crease at the corner of his mouth. He turned and spit into a coffee can beside the stove and looked back at Wayne, wiping a grimy arm across his mouth.

"What do they call you?"

The man's appearance and manner irritated Wayne. He answered: "Mostly they just call me 'kid'."

The answer caught the slovenly herder off guard and he reddened. "Well, my name's Pat Unger, and not ashamed of it. Where you from?"

Increasingly reluctant to tell this man anything, Wayne replied: "I just hailed into Waltman."

Unger spat again, mostly into the can. "Well, now, ain't that somethin'? He's a kid and he just hailed in. Well let me tell you something, Kid Hailer, or whatever cute name you want to call yourself, you start playing tough guy around here you're going to get your little baby face rubbed right in the dirt."

When Wayne failed to answer he shrugged his shoulders and bristled over to his bunk and flopped down on it. As he did Wayne noticed it was the only dirty bunk in the place. Another partly full spit-can stood beside it. The brown stain on the floor attested to the carelessness of his aim.

Ignoring him, Wayne went back to straightening his bedroll, rolling his heavy coat at the head for a pillow. The name the slovenly herder had tagged onto him kept rolling around in his mind. 'Kid Hailer,' he thought. 'That ain't bad! Everyone always calls me "Kid" anyway. Maybe I'll just let 'em call me "Kid Hailer".'

He turned his head as the door opened again. One of the men Curt had sent to help Lessman stood just inside the door. He was lean and dark, with a flat-crowned hat that

29

looked out of place in Wyoming. He walked over, showing yellowed teeth in a big smile, and held out his hand. In a heavily accented voice he said, "Keed, you come at pretty bad time, do pretty good job. My name is Pete Alvarez. Boss, he say maybe we work together for lambing. You green hand with sheep, eh?"

Wayne smiled back and warmed with the firm grip of the other's hand. "Yeah, I'm plumb green with sheep." Then without even thinking he asked, "You Spanish?"

Pete's grin broadened. "Not Spanish. Me Mex. Mexican. I come from Guadalupe."

"That's a long ways, isn't it?"

"*Si*. I work long time on Rancho Taos. Then Curt, he come looking for men that know sheeps, and I hire on. I know sheeps real good. You want to herd sheep, I teach you."

Wayne liked him instinctively. There was a bubbling warm sincerity that flowed out from him that made Wayne

30

feel accepted and comfortable. They sat together at one of the small tables looking out the window, and Pete began to fill him in.

"Winter bands coming in now," he explained. "We go down to three bands for winter, maybe fifteen hundred, one thousand sheeps in each band. Coming in now for to have their lambs."

Wayne began to quiz him. "Is lambing pretty tough work?"

Pete leaned across the table. "Lambing time is very great time!" His enthusiasm beamed. "It is great time to see the lambs being born, to watch the mothers taking care of them. It is a beautiful thing."

Unger spoke from his bunk. "Don't let him lie to you, Kid. You work yourself clear into the ground during lambing."

Pete thought about it for a minute, then continued: "It is work, too, *si*. Much work. If weather is good, it is good time, though."

Wayne countered. "But what if the

weather isn't good?"

Pete's face darkened slightly. "Then that is more work. If we have storm we have to work in shelter as much as we can. The ewes, they don't like to claim their lambs then, and it is hard."

The supper bell jangled so they walked together to the ranch house. The food was good and plentiful. Wayne remembered he hadn't eaten since the night before and he finished his third plateful before he pushed back. Several of the hands had pulled out bags of Bull Durham and rolled cigarettes when Curt came in with Scotty.

Scotty took a place at the end of the table and began filling his plate while Curt spoke to the men. "Boys," he began without preliminaries. "I think we got trouble. Guess you probably met the kid by now. Boss hired him in Waltman. They got jumped on the way home. Fella hidin' in the clump of aspens above Dry Crick shot through the windshield. He hit the boss and woulda got the kid too if he hadn't been quite so quick. Anyway the kid killed him and brought the boss home."

Several heads turned to look at Wayne, then a hand named Morgan spoke up. "Who was he?"

Curt shook his head. "Don't know. Me'n Scotty went up there and buried him. Hadn't never seen him before. We turned his horse loose."

Another hand spoke up. "Horse have a brand?"

Silence fell instant and complete as they waited Curt's answer. "FX. Fox's brand."

As one the assembled hands expelled their breath in a rush, and a babble of voices erupted as each man began to talk with the man next to him. After a minute Curt held up his hand for silence, and the babble of voices slowly subsided.

When it was quiet he said, "I don't know what Fox has on his mind. There's been others try to run sheep outfits out, from time to time. I don't expect nothin' like that Johnson County thing up north a few years ago, but herders alone are goin' to have to watch themselves. If any of you want to draw your pay I won't blame you none."

Pat Unger stood at once. "I'll take that and a ride to town first thing tomorrow. I didn't hire out to fight no war. I ain't sure I can stand them stinkin' sheep no more nohow, and I sure ain't gonna fight for 'em."

As he stomped out a hand at the far end of the room spoke quietly, but his voice carried easily to everyone in the room. "Well, that'll make the bunkhouse smell better, if nothin' else."

Several of the men laughed but Curt's expression never changed. He turned to Wayne. "Kid, I don't know nothin' about you. You rode for the brand right enough today, but the same offer goes for you. If you want out, the boss'll give you a month's pay and a ride back to town."

Wayne's face reflected his surprise.

34

"No, I don't guess I want to quit. Not unless you want to get rid of me 'cause I killed that guy."

Curt answered quickly. "Not that at all. That was him or you, and he opened up first. Spent shell was still in his rifle, and you hit him in the chest from the front. I just don't want you feelin' crowded into a fight that ain't yours."

Without waiting any further answer he turned and walked into the adjoining room, but they could still hear him talking. "Mrs. Lessman? Is Bill awake?"

It was Lessman himself that answered. "I'm awake. I been listenin'. I'll be in bed a few days, but I'm too gol-dangled mean to stay long. By jing I thought I was bringing home a kid to raise, but he sure saved my bacon, didn't he?"

A couple of hands chuckled appreciatively, and Wayne felt his face redden again. He got up and went outside, furious with himself. "Why did I have to get such a baby face?" he asked himself angrily. "Life would sure be a lot easier if I didn't keep blushing all the time like some schoolgirl."

He went back to the bunkhouse and turned in, but lay awake far into the night before falling asleep. They had just finished breakfast the next morning when he heard the first band of sheep approaching, so he went to the corral to watch. He was dumbfounded and breathed, "One man is expected to herd that many sheep?"

It looked like a sea of dirty white moving across the flat, with black spots floating in random splashes of colour. The herder sat his horse to one side watching, and Wayne realized at once it was the dogs, not the herder, that controlled the sheep. He forgot everything in his fascination with the poetry of those sheep dogs. An old ewe broke from the herd behind one of the dogs. As though sensing what he couldn't see the dog wheeled in almost the same instant to circle and crowd her back into the herd. An old ram turned to challenge him, and the dog

36

circled behind and carefully nipped his rump to change his mind, then hazed him back into the band.

The herder loped his horse to the gate of the huge corral and opened it, then moved away. He stood in his stirrups and gave a sharp whistle. The dogs both stopped in their tracks and stood looking at him. Removing his hat he swung it in a wide sweeping motion that ended at his chest. Instantly both dogs broke into action and began to move the band of sheep through the gate.

Wayne gasped. "I don't believe it!"

Pete chuckled beside him. "You never seen dogs work before?"

Wayne replied, "We always had a good cow-dog, but nothing like that! How do they know what to do?"

Pete pointed at the herder, sitting his horse. "Herder tell them. Hat sign. Way he move his hat tell dogs what to do. Brown dog is Mickey. If he can't see herder to see what to do, he will stand on back legs and jump to see what herder say with hat."

Wayne's amazement deepened. "How do they get trained like that?"

Pete's smile widened into a grin of pride. "I teach them. I train two, three dogs for each herder. Teach herders how to use them. Good dog make even green kid good herder. Without dog, good herder can't handle band of sheep. They are too many."

Wayne responded. "I always thought of my horse that way, but never a dog."

Pete looked at him gravely. "Is important. Cowboy take care of horse, then himself. Sheep-herder take care of dogs, then horse, then self."

When the sheep were in the corral and the gate shut the herder rode into the yard and dismounted beside Curt. "Well, there they are, Curt," he said. "They're all yours. You got a ride goin' into town today or tomorrow? I ain't been to town for five months and I'm sure due to find me a bottle and a woman and a bath. In that order."

Curt chuckled. "Smells to me like you better find the bath first. You can go up to the house and draw your pay. The other two herders will most likely want to go too, so we'll go in tomorrow. You want a job again, look me or Lessman up."

Wayne's face reflected his confusion. He turned to Pete when the herder had moved off to take care of his horse. "What do they do, just quit when they go to town?"

"*Si*. They go to town, get drunk, stay drunk until they run out of money. Then they pawn their watch and their saddle and maybe their guns, and stay drunk until they are out of money again. Then they find whoever need hands and hire on."

"What about the stuff they pawn? How do they get it back?"

"New boss get their stuff and take them to ranch. They work till they ready to go to town again. When boss pay wages he keep money he give pawn shop."

"Don't they ever hire back to the same outfit?"

"Oh, *si*, sometimes. Mostly that is when a man get married. Then he live in one of those houses and stay with one outfit. I think a wife is a good thing."

Wayne asked, "You ever been married?"

Pete sighed. "No, *amigo*. Someday I marry pretty *señorita*, have little band of sheep and big band of kids. I save money. I wait. Pretty soon go back to Guadalupe, then not be so lonesome like here."

Wayne thought about it for a minute, and for some reason he couldn't fathom, the face of the boss's daughter framed itself in his mind. He asked Pete, "What's that girl's name? The one that came outside to help Lessman?"

Pete's eyes danced. "Ah, yes, I see you keep looking after she had gone, at the spot where she was. She is a pretty *señorita*. Her name is LaDonna. She is very much girl. She work like man when they need her, and is nice to hands. She make somebody very fine wife."

Wayne felt his face redden again. Furious with himself he wheeled and walked back to the bunkhouse, but he couldn't get that face out of his mind.

3

THAT afternoon the other two bands of sheep came into the valley and were held close. The next day the shearers came. For the next two weeks they were all busy from dark to dark, sorting, holding, shearing, and packing wool. Wayne was assigned to the wool-packing in the barn. As the sheep were sheared the wool was taken to the barn and bagged in the biggest burlap bags he had ever seen. They were hung from the rafters of the barn, with the top of the bag just above the floor of the hay mow. When the bag was half-full Wayne would jump down into it and tramp the wool as it was dumped in. He kept tramping until the bag was full and he was back up to the level of the hay mow. Then the bag was stitched shut and a new bag was hung. The full bags were stacked in one end of the barn to wait for the wool buyers who would check, grade, and weigh the wool, then dicker with Lessman for a price.

After they were sheared the sheep looked naked, cold, and skinny. Each had a bright red 'Rocking R' painted on its back, and the bands of sheep looked like dirty fields of snow splattered with blood. The thought was disquieting to him, and he shrugged it off. As he leaned on the top rail of the corral watching them, he felt someone beside him and turned. It was LaDonna.

"Oh! Uh, hi. I didn't see you walk up," he stammered.

She smiled at his awkwardness and looked toward the sheep. "You were too busy watching the sheep. I always think they look so little and cold after they've been sheared."

He responded, "Yeah, I was just thinking that too. How's your dad?"

She turned to face him and looked at him seriously. "He's better. The fever's gone. The day after he buried the gunman, Curt went into Waltman and got the doctor. He cleaned the wound and gave Dad some medicine. He'll be OK."

He started to say something but she laid a hand on his arm, stopping him. "Wayne, I know you saved his life. I want you to know I appreciate that, very much."

He blushed again and couldn't think of anything to say that didn't sound dumb. He finally said, "Aw, I guess I just did what anybody would have."

She didn't pursue the matter. She said, "I hope you stay on here."

They talked for a while and she went back to the house. He went to the bunkhouse with the words echoing circles in his head. "I hope you stay on here."

Two weeks later the first of the ewes began to lamb. It went well for several days, and Wayne learned more about sheep than he thought there was to know. Pete taught him tricks to get a reluctant ewe to accept her lambs that he never would have thought of, and he was constantly surprised at the man's store of knowledge. He actually began to like the sheep, and to recognize varying personality patterns among them. It was hard work and long hours, but he was enjoying it.

Then the storm struck. All day they had watched the black clouds building and their line advancing across the sky. Just after noon the wind shifted and began to blow cold and wet. Pete nodded at the sky. "We are in for trouble, *amigo*. Bad storm come."

By supper time the snow had started. The wind, full in the north-east now, was picking up, while the temperature dropped steadily. After supper Wayne went to the bunkhouse and put on an extra pair of longjohns and a third pair of socks. He knotted a second neckerchief around his neck, turned up the collar of his heavy coat, and put on mittens. The storm had grown noticeably worse even while he was inside doing that.

That night it seemed like every ewe that was within two weeks of her time decided to lamb. By midnight the wind and snow were whipping so badly Wayne couldn't see a ewe until he was within ten feet of her, so he had to keep moving all around the collected bands. When a ewe would have a lamb he had to stand it on its feet on the sheltered side of the ewe to try to get its belly full of warm milk. Often he had to tie the ewe immovably so she would let it feed. While that one fed, he'd find another and do the same. Then he had to hurry back to free the first one before she froze to death from standing still.

All night long the storm continued, and all night long Wayne and Pete worked side by side. They knew that out of sight in the fury of the storm every other hand was doing the same. Morning brought a lightening of the air but not of the storm. By noon two and a half feet of snow lay on the ground, and the exhausted crew took turns going in to eat and return.

Wayne worked in a near stupor. His legs and arms were numb. His toes and fingers ached with cold. His hands moved in slow-motion clumsiness. His world was reduced to a ten-foot circle of visibility in an endless swirling universe of white. He lost all track of time, performing his job in an endless repetition.

All afternoon it continued. Supper, like breakfast and dinner, was eaten in shifts. By midnight the storm began to lessen, and exhausted men staggered to the bunkhouse by twos and threes to sleep for four hours, then return to spell somebody else.

When Wayne's turn came for rest he was so tired he could hardly open the bunkhouse door. He started to climb into his bed fully dressed, but an older hand stopped him. "You don't want to do that kid," he warned. "Give your body and your clothes both a chance. Hang your clothes on that rope by the stove so's they'll dry. You'll sleep warmer too."

47

Wayne knew he was right. With leaden movements he peeled off the wet and frozen layers of clothing and hung them by the fire. He climbed into his bunk and was asleep before his head hit the mattress.

He was sure it was just an instant later an insistent hand on his shoulder shook him awake. It was Morgan, still dressed, his handle-bar moustache hanging heavy and twice its size with ice and frost. "Four hours are up, Kid. Time to roll out. Cook's got a bait of grub ready for you at the house 'fore you head back to the lambin' pens."

As Morgan undressed and collapsed into bed, Wayne forced his reluctant body to respond. His arms and legs felt like they were made of lead. His mouth was dry and foul-tasting. His mind was in a fog that he couldn't seem to fight through. Slowly he retrieved his clothes from the rope by the stove.

As he struggled into his clothes he was suddenly grateful that the older hand had insisted on his undressing.

His clothes were dry and warm. With breakfast and four cups of scalding coffee in him, he felt almost human again when he got back to the lambing corral to start another shift.

Almost a week later the weather turned warm again. By that time the lambing was nearly done, and life had taken on a more normal pace. As they left the lambing corral one evening Pete stopped in the middle of the yard and looked hard at Wayne for a full minute. "Keed," he said, "you best green hand I ever see. I tell boss you want to take band to the mountain, you do good."

Wayne glowed. "Thanks, Pete," he blushed. "I'd like that."

The words filled Wayne with a warmth that surprised him. He hadn't realized how much he missed his father's frequent words of approval and encouragement. He needed the acceptance of this new world. He hungered to know he belonged, that he fit in. The approval he thirsted for was doubly sweet when it came because he knew he had earned it. For the first time he felt confidence that maybe he could handle a band of sheep on the mountains.

The days that followed allowed the crew to rest and recuperate from the taxing pace of lambing. As Wayne strolled into the bunkhouse one afternoon he sensed an air of expectancy, and looked around to find its source. It seemed everybody was looking at him. Paul O'Connell, a burly Irishman hired for lambing, stood up. He laughed once, without humour. "Sure, Kid, and 'tis you we was just talkin' of. I'm thinkin' you're a two-bit brown-noser."

Wayne's face flushed red and his blue eyes flashed and went flat and pale. "What're you talkin' about?" he asked.

"'Tis you I'm talkin' about!" the Irishman bristled. "Sure an' they're just now giving me my time because they're havin' enough herders for the summer. I'm sayin' you been brown-nosin' that

Mexican so he gives you a band instead o' me that's been herdin' sheep in this country for fourteen years."

Wayne stood his ground. "If Pete thinks I'm a better man I guess that's just how it'll have to be."

O'Connell's face went livid. His shoulders hunched and his voice shook as he pointed a finger at Wayne. "Sure and no snot-nosed kid from nowhere is takin' a herdin' job from Paul O'Connell! If you're thinkin' to live another day you'll be gettin' your time and leavin' here, boy. Are you hearin' me now?"

Wayne was looking Paul over as they talked, really seeing him for the first time. He was a powerful man, with shoulders that tapered almost straight up to his ears, making it appear that he didn't have a neck. His ears lay flat against the sides of his massive head, and his forehead protruded out over flashing eyes. His hands were huge, and Wayne knew if this man ever got a hold on him he could squeeze the

51

life out of him as easily as squashing a ripe tomato.

The red flush in Wayne's face deepened from his collar up across his face. The muscles on his jaw bunched as he clenched his teeth and his eyes flashed fire. The thin line of his lips scarcely moved as he spoke softly: "If the boss says you're laid off, I guess you're laid off. You better just leave it that way or this snot-nosed kid'll have to take a fall out of you."

With an angry bellow Paul ducked his head and lunged forward, diving to catch hold of Wayne. Wayne sidestepped and grabbed Paul by the hair and belt as he went by, forcing his head into the side of the heavy cast-iron heating stove with the full weight of his lunging body behind it.

The stove tipped over with the impact. The stove, Paul, the stove-pipe, and a cloud of black soot crashed in a pile. To Wayne's surprise Paul lunged to his feet with a roar, blood mixing with the soot and running out of his hair. He swung a startlingly fast right that Wayne almost didn't move quickly enough to evade. It grazed his temple but he stepped in behind it and let loose with a quick left and right into Paul's face, then ducked away. The blows were solid and the flesh split beneath them, opening a large gash on both of Paul's cheekbones, but they seemed to have no effect at all.

He lunged after Wayne, landing a glancing blow across his mouth. Again Wayne stepped in behind it, hit twice, and ducked away. The crew watched silently, not interfering. Wayne was sure they wouldn't interfere, either for him or against him. In this country a man rode his own broncs and fought his own fights, win lose or draw. The salty taste of his own blood swam in his mouth and his ears were filled with roaring. He fought the lunging Paul skilfully, landing a constant barrage of blows while staying mostly out of Paul's reach, but his blows seemed to have no effect at all.

They continued the pattern of the battle. Lunge and dodge. Hit and duck away. Then Wayne's foot caught the threshold and he fell out the door backward. With a roar Paul leaped to land atop him, but Wayne got his feet up in time to use Paul's momentum to propel him over into the yard.

With an amazing agility Paul gained his feet first. As Wayne rolled to hands and knees Paul caught him squarely in the ribs with a solid kick. The force of the kick lifted Wayne clear of the ground and he felt ribs snap with the impact. Fighting for breath he let the force of the kick roll him an extra turn and he came to his feet with Paul right after him. He side-stepped and dodged, fighting for time to regain his wind. He felt the stabbing pain of broken ribs with each gasp for air.

He remembered a ruse his father had used once. He gave a groan and dropped to one knee, holding his hurt side. Paul recognized it as the effect of the kick and stopped, planting his feet for another kick. As he stopped, Wayne came up from the ground, driving a straight right hand to the point of Paul's chin with all the force of his legs as well as his arm behind it. The blow landed with a dull 'thunk'. The shock of it travelled the length of Wayne's arm, shooting such a stab of pain through his side he nearly collapsed.

Paul's eyes momentarily crossed, and Wayne recovered his balance to send a left hook into Paul's jaw with everything he had on it. He felt the jawbone crunch beneath his fist, but Paul just stood there. Panic surged Wayne's mind. "What do I have to do to knock this man down?"

He set his feet to deliver another straight right when he saw Paul start to topple. He stepped back, and Paul slowly tipped forward like a great tree before the axe. He hit the ground with a thud, dust splaying out from around him. He did not move.

Wayne sat down abruptly on the ground, his strength gone. He needed not to breathe, because his side hurt so much with every breath. At the same time his winded body demanded breath in great gulps, so he sat there alternately gasping for breath and wincing in pain.

When he had recovered enough breath, he struggled to his feet and went to the pump. Pumping water into the trough he dunked his head, and was surprised to see the water turn red. He couldn't remember getting hit the number of times he must have been. His lips were split and bleeding. His nose was flattened and bleeding. His left eye was already swollen shut, with blood running from both above and below it. He had lumps on his head and both jaws. His ribs hurt with each breath. He wanted to lie down and die, but he straightened instead. He would rather die than let the crew see him surrender to pain.

He stood as straight as he could and walked back to where Paul was just beginning to stir. As he got to his hands and knees he shook his head to try to clear it. Through thick lips Wayne slurred, "You still think I'm a snot-nosed kid? If you do get up and we'll finish this."

Paul struggled to his feet. He looked at Wayne from a face that looked like a rounded mass of raw meat. He took a ragged breath and answered heavily, "Kid, sure and you hit like a mule kicks. It's been for bein' a long time since Paul O'Connell's been whipped, but I'm whipped."

Wayne heaved a sigh of relief and headed for the bunkhouse. If Paul had wanted more fight he didn't know where he could have found the strength to give it to him. He couldn't remember it ever hurting so much to win!

When he woke the next morning he started to roll off his bunk and cried out in the sudden memory of broken ribs. Carefully he eased off the bunk and found more sources of pain than he had parts of his body. He looked up at a low chuckle, and looked into the most battered face he had ever seen.

Paul faced him with a twisted grin on a grotesquely swollen face. One eye was swollen shut and the other nearly so. His nose was three times its normal size. One side of his face was swollen so far it looked like his head must surely fall over sideways. Both ears were split and swollen until they looked like giant warts on the sides of his head. He spoke through lips so inflated they seemed scarcely to move. "Sure Kid, and your look would be makin' the babies cry!"

"Yeah, I suppose," Wayne retorted. "Have you looked at yourself?"

"Sure an' I have, Kid. An' it told me the truth of what I'm feelin', that you whipped me fair and you whipped me good. Sure and 'tis my hand I'm offerin' you now."

He held out a swollen hand and Wayne took it gingerly. "Proud to, long as you don't squeeze too hard. Hittin' you is like hittin' a brick wall!"

"Sure, an' I've been told that before, I have, but never by a man that whipped me. The boss is for takin' me to Waltman. He thinks the doctor will be wirin' my jaw shut. I'm thinkin' your ribs could stand for him to be lookin' at them too."

Wayne took a deep breath and agreed. "Might be a good idea. I'd hate to have one of 'em poke a hole in my lung. If it ain't already."

He dressed and they grimaced their way to the Model 'T' Lessman had started. The last thing the grinning crew heard was two voices groaning in unison when the car hit a bump at the edge of the yard.

When Wayne and Lessman returned without Paul it was late and the crew was asleep.

4

THE wounds of battle were nearly healed when the Sky Pilot came. Wayne had been working with Pete every day, getting used to the dogs and learning to work them. The dogs responded well to him, and he came to appreciate them more every day. Once he saw a coyote sneaking up on a ewe with twin lambs at the fringes of the band. He reached for his rifle, but Pete stopped him.

"No shoot," he cautioned. "Scare sheeps. Watch."

As they watched, Mickey caught the coyote's scent. He barked one short, sharp bark, and began running. Flat out, belly to the ground, he looked like a blur streaking through the sage brush. The coyote heard his approach and wheeled to face him. They locked in a furious struggle, and the coyote seemed to be getting the better of the fight. Suddenly the coyote was bowled to the side by the furry shape of Runt, rocketing from nowhere into his right flank. The coyote yelped a startled and hurt squeal and whirled to find his new attacker. As his attention diverted he was grasped by the throat in Mickey's jaw.

As he tried to whirl back to rinse the fangs from his throat, Runt struck again. Reaching under the coyote he grabbed the off hind leg and jerked it under and behind the coyote. Thrown from his feet by the manoeuvre, the coyote tried vainly to jerk his hind leg free.

With his throat in the jaws of one dog and his hind leg in the jaws of another, the coyote twisted and jerked frantically until his torn jugular had spewed his strength and speed across the greening buffalo grass. With a gasping rattle he ceased his struggles.

The dogs continued their furious snarling and pulling until they realized they were only fighting the pull of each other. They released their grip and the lifeless body of the coyote lay on the ground. Panting, they stood for a moment, then Runt wheeled and trotted back to the band that had moved nervously away, while Mickey lay down to lick his wounds and savour the victory.

Wayne watched with a curious mixture of feelings. He felt a strange sympathy for the coyote, starved into carelessness and risk at the end of a hard winter. He felt almost a revulsion against the vicious attack of the dogs that killed so quickly and cruelly. At the same time he felt a fierce pride that they so efficiently protected their charges. They were cruel in their efficiency, but they were magnificent! They herded and fought like a precision machine. Wayne knew it was that same mixture of pride and a dozen other emotions that gave Pete's voice its huskiness.

"They good dogs, those two. Good dogs."

They were still standing there, still a little awed, when Curly called from the horse corral. "Somebody's comin'. He's afoot."

They walked quickly back to the yard where the hands were gathering to watch. From the north-east a lone figure could be made out, walking the ridges away from the snow that still lay deep in the bottoms. He walked with a long swinging stride. As he drew closer they could begin to hear strange wisps of sound. It was Scotty that recognized it.

"He's singing! He's afoot, and he's singing!"

Vance Morgan spit on the ground. "Aw, it's that Sky Pilot. He come through here last fall. He just walks all over this country."

He turned and stomped toward the bunkhouse, but the rest of the hands stayed where they were, watching the advancing figure. They talked as they watched.

"What's a Sky Pilot doin' in this country?"

"How come he's walkin'?"

"Ain't got no horse, I reckon."

"What's he want?"

"Wanted us to have church last fall."

"Church?"

"Uh huh. Moved the tables outa the chow hall and set the chairs up, and had a reg'lar church service. He done most o' the singin' but the women joined in pretty good, and some o' the men. Some of the boys knowed them songs real good."

"What'd he preach?"

"Oh, just preachin'."

"Sure walks good, don't he? Don't see how a man can walk like that."

"He walked in last fall. When he left, he walked out, headin' north. Musta found somebody to take him in for the winter."

"S'pose he walks in the winter too?"

"Not unless he's got snowshoes!"

The conversation continued until the man approached the yard. His appearance became more striking as

64

he neared. He was a tall man, standing six-foot-two or three, but he was skinny as a scarecrow. His long neck jutted forward, giving his head a heavy and ungainly appearance. He had a pack attached to his back with a bedroll tied across the bottom and a rifle lashed to the side. His hands were empty. As he walked he swung his arms back and forth in wide flopping swings that gave him a comical, not-quite-human appearance. He sang in a rich baritone that seemed to float above him like a detached spectre of sound accompanying him.

As he walked into the yard, Lessman stepped out onto the porch. "Evenin', Reverend. I see you survived the winter."

The Sky Pilot grinned. "Indeed I did! Good evening Mrs. Lessman, Mr. Lessman. Good evening, men. How did lambing go this year?"

The men mumbled greetings. A couple of them touched the brim of their hats as though undecided whether they should remove them. Lessman answered his question. "We did very well. That one bad storm caught us right in the middle, but the men stayed with it and we weathered it pretty good. Didn't lose hardly any."

"Wonderful!" The Sky Pilot nodded. "So glad to hear it. And how are you getting along? I heard you had been wounded."

"Word gets around, doesn't it? It's healing well. I'm not riding any broncs yet, but it's about healed. Come on in, come in. You must be tired."

They walked together into the house and their voices faded as the men turned back to the bunkhouse.

"What day's today?"

"Danged if I know. Friday. Saturday, maybe."

"Saturday. Betcha the Sky Pilot's gonna have church tomorrow."

"Well, you don't gotta go, you don't wanta."

"Oh, I'll go. Ain't nothin' better to do nohow. 'Sides, I don't wanta get the boss sore at me."

"He ain't gonna get sore at you. He ain't never told nobody they gotta go. Sky Pilot comes by, we have church. That's all."

"He one of them dunkers?"

"Yup. Anyone thinks he wants baptized, the Sky Pilot dunks 'em over at the big hole on the crick."

"Ever see anyone get dunked?"

"Yeah, a couple. Wasn't that much to it, near as I could see. Sure seemed to make a change in 'em, though."

The bunkhouse door burst open and Morgan came in carrying an old saddle. It was covered with dust and pieces of hay clung to it. The skirts were curled under and stiff as a board. The leather covering was gone from the stirrup irons, and they were rusty. The leather was worn from the front edge of the saddle-horn, and the steel of the horn showed through. He sat it on one of the empty tables where nobody was playing cards.

"What are you doin' with that relic,

Morgan?" one of the hands called out. "That thing's been ridin' a stall fence in the barn since before the first time I worked here."

Morgan's big moustache lifted above a tobacco stained grin. "Why, fellas, I'm gettin' set to fix this fine saddle. I got me some Neatsfoot Oil, and some saddle soap, and I'm gonna soften this leather up, and freshen it up, and make a real fine saddle out of this."

"Yeah? For what?"

"Why fellas, I'm plumb surprised at you. Ain't it never occurred to you that it just ain't right for a Sky Pilot to be on foot? We're just gonna have to fix that man up with a saddle and a good horse, now, to it!"

Some of the men grinned and exchanged knowing looks as they went back to what they were doing. The pungent smell of Neatsfoot Oil permeated the air. Morgan was still working vigorously on his project when Wayne drifted off to sleep.

The next morning began routinely.

When the chores were finished the men went in to breakfast. They were just finishing when Lessman came into the chow hall. "Men," he announced, "today's Sunday, and the Sky Pilot's here. We'll have church today for any of you that wants to come. We'll clear this room and just put the benches in rows. Anyone wants to clean up, you can, but you don't have to. You can come or not to suit yourself. Only thing I ask is you treat the Sky Pilot with respect. He deserves that, whether you agree with him or not, and he'll get it as long as he's on my outfit. We won't be doin' no other work today."

He went back into the house and men began to move the tables. They put the tables all against one wall of the long room and arranged the benches in rows in the remaining space. Then they went outside to mill around and smoke while they waited.

When Curt and Art and their wives came from their houses, Wayne's mouth dropped open in surprise. Both men were decked out in broadcloth suits, ruffled shirts, and string ties. Their wives wore dresses that looked to Wayne like they just stepped out of the mail order catalogue. He hadn't recovered from that when Pete and Curly came from the bunkhouse. Curly wore a broadcloth suit much like Curt's, but Pete was resplendent. He was dressed in a white shirt and black trousers, with a short black jacket. Across the shoulders and down the arms of the jacket was a row of silver spangles. A matching row of spangles made a straight line down the outside of each pants leg. The front and back of the jacket was covered with silver embroidery and shining sequins. His boots shone with a gleam the yard's dust couldn't cover. The men whistled and bowed and whooped as the men crossed the yard, and both men grinned in response.

Wayne was surprised that every hand on the place came to church. Morgan and Scotty were last to arrive, and their faces were flushed. They slid quickly into chairs and carefully studied their hands. Several of the men turned to look at them, then at one another, and their eyes twinkled.

Morgan and Scotty had scarcely gotten into their chairs when the Sky Pilot came in. He began without announcement to sing 'Holy, Holy, Holy'. The women picked it up at once, and one by one the men's voices began to blend in. They went from song to song, following the Sky Pilot's lead, with no song being announced. They sang one verse of each one, and Wayne was again surprised at how many of the men knew a lot of the words. He himself knew almost none of them, but enjoyed listening.

When the Sky Pilot thought they had sung enough he launched directly into his sermon. Afterward Wayne tried to remember what he had said, but couldn't remember much. There was one thing from the sermon that stuck with him, though. It rankled in him for a long time. He could even remember the man's tone and the look on his face as he had said it.

"There's something in us that's out of tune with the Almighty," he said. "When we feel guilt for our tears, feel shame if we blush, feel regret if we show mercy, but feel nothing when we beat another man senseless, or take the life of another human being."

Wayne wondered, "Is he talking about me?" But he saw the others squirming just as uncomfortably, and he knew he wasn't being singled out. Nevertheless the words stuck in his mind.

He might have gotten more out of the sermon if LaDonna hadn't been there. He was sitting one row behind and just a little beside her, and he couldn't keep his eyes away. Her radiant red hair cascaded across the shoulders of a rich green dress with rows of lace down the front and around the sleeves. She sang with a rich voice and moved with such grace that Wayne was startled into remembrance of where he was several times. He simply became so entranced watching her that his surroundings disappeared. It was a wonder he remembered any of that sermon!

As the service drew to a close his attention again strayed to Morgan. He was puzzled. He knew Morgan was not even remotely religious, yet he sat through the entire service. He sat rigidly straight on the bench, turning his hat in his hands constantly. Wayne also picked up the air of expectancy in several others as they glanced repeatedly toward Morgan and Scotty. Wayne soon drew a conclusion that the church service was not the only attraction of the day.

As soon as the service was finished Morgan and Scotty, trailed by two of the others, walked up to the Sky Pilot, hats in hand. It was Morgan who addressed him. "Uh, Rever'nd, we surely do appreciate your comin' here and all, bringin' us religion and that. Well, we'd like to show our appreciation, so we'd like for you to come on out to the corral. We got somethin' we'd like to give ya."

The Sky Pilot looked from face to face, but before he could answer the four men facing him turned and walked out, so he followed. The rest of them, women and all, fell into step behind him. Wayne looked at Lessman. His face had turned red and he opened his mouth to call out something, then shut it again. The muscles along the line of his jaw were knotted and his forehead was pulled down over his eyes. He pressed his lips tightly and kept pace with the others.

Followed first by the Sky Pilot, then by the entire procession, Morgan and the others walked directly to the horse corral. Tied to the 'snubbing post', the large post set directly in the centre of the round corral, was a horse Wayne hadn't seen before. It was wearing the saddle Morgan had worked on long into the night.

As they approached the corral Morgan opened the gate for the Sky Pilot. The others climbed the fence to sit on the top rail. The women stood outside, looking between the rails. Morgan was talking.

"Now, me and the boy's was a-talkin' and we decided it just ain't fittin' for you to be walkin' all the time, bein' a man o' the cloth, and all. So we kinda went together and figured to buy this outfit off of the boss and give it to you, so's you wouldn't need to walk."

The Sky Pilot looked over the horse as they talked. As they neared him he rolled his eyes and pulled back hard against the snubbing rope. His ears lay back flat against his head, and his sides trembled. His feet were pawing against the ground as he strained against his tether. The Sky Pilot's eyes danced as he spoke.

"He seems a bit nervous, wouldn't you say?"

"Aw, he's just high-spirited. Man

of your position oughta have a high-spirited horse, not just some nag."

"I see. Is he well broken?"

Morgan nearly sputtered, then caught himself. "Why, nearly every hand on the place has been on him, one time or another."

"Ah, yes. Does he have a name?"

"Uh, well, I guess some of the boys call him 'Twister', but I guess maybe, uh, 'Red' might be a better name."

"Twister. My, that's a powerful name, isn't it?"

"I reckon he's a powerful horse all right. He'll stand up to a lot o' ridin'."

The Sky Pilot smiled. "I'm sure he will. Now it would be an insult to mount such a handsome animal with my Sunday shoes on, wouldn't it? You're about my size, Morgan. Would you mind lending me your boots?"

As Morgan hesitated Scotty spoke up from the corral fence. "Rever'nd, I got a pair I brung along with me that oughta just fit you. I thought may be it'd be better was you wearin' boots."

He tossed a pair of boots into the corral, and the horse shied violently from the sudden move. The Sky Pilot grinned openly. "Well, now, that was certainly thoughtful of you, Scotty, isn't it? Thank you."

He walked to the side of the corral and leaned against the fence to change shoes. He handed his Sunday shoes up to Scotty, and Morgan untied the horse. As he approached, Morgan took a firm grip on the hackamore, but the Sky Pilot took the reins.

"Thank you, Morgan. Perhaps I can handle the reins."

As Morgan moved away and climbed the fence the Sky Pilot talked softly to the horse until he began to settle down. Carefully he fed the right rein across the horse's neck, then taking both reins in his left hand he gripped them together with a handful of the horse's mane. Still talking softly, he reached his right hand to grip the left stirrup. He twisted it around to face him. He thrust his left foot into the stirrup and in a swift and fluid motion grabbed the saddle-horn with his right hand and swung into the saddle.

As his weight hit the stirrup the horse tensed, but the Sky Pilot's left hand was pulling the reins hard. The only direction the horse's first motion could go was to circle toward the mounting rider. His motion moved him right under the Sky Pilot as he swung into the saddle, and his right foot found the stirrup. As his foot slid into that stirrup he let the reins slack, leaned back, slapped the horse resoundingly on the rump, and let out a yell that caused the assembled audience to jump violently.

The entire manoeuvre took a fraction of a second, but the startled horse reacted immediately. With a squeal he exploded. He took two running steps then jumped straight into the air, humping his back and ducking his head between his front legs. The action left the saddle and rider perched on the top of a tilting circle of his back. At the top of his jump he twisted his head sharply to the left and kicked with both hind feet. The effect of the plunge and kick snapped the rider's back, and his head lashed backward like the tip of a whip. An instant later the horse's front feet hit the ground with a bone-jarring shock.

As his feet struck the ground the horse twisted the opposite direction and left the ground in another leap higher than the first. At the apex of the jump he reversed the twist and kicked as before. At the top of the second jump, as the horse kicked, the Sky Pilot let out another yell that sounded like, "Yeeeehaaaah!"

The assembled crew watched open-mouthed. They had thought they were going to watch a greenhorn get 'stacked up'. In one of the oldest stunts of the range they had put what they thought was a greenhorn on one of the roughest broncs the ranch owned, for the sheer delight of watching him get bucked off. After he was bucked off, if he took it as a joke, they would help him up, brush him off, and accept him as a good sport. If he failed to take it as a joke he would become the brunt of every conceivable shenanigan as long as he remained.

This time however, the joke was on them. It was obvious from the first jump the horse made that this was no greenhorn. Scotty was the first to respond. "Look at him ride!" he yelled. "Ride 'im, Preacher!"

At once the rest took up the cry, and the watchers became an enthusiastic cheering section, yelling and waving their hats.

The horse was strong, and he continued to buck for nearly fifteen minutes. When his strength was spent and he had failed to unseat his rider, he came to a halt. He stood, spraddle-legged and trembling in the swirling dust. The Sky Pilot let him stand for half a minute, then nudged him gently with his spurs. The horse gave another half-hearted jump, then stopped again.

The rider nudged him again, and he began to walk in mincing steps that were half walk and half jump. The Sky Pilot kept him moving, walking this way and that across the corral. Tired and hot as he was, he could not be allowed to stand still. If he did, his muscles would knot and cramp, he would cool too quickly, and he would be ruined.

When the Sky Pilot had walked the horse sufficiently, he stopped and stepped down. Morgan jumped down from the fence, and he handed him the reins. He smiled and spoke in a voice easily heard by the whole group.

"That is a fine horse, Morgan. I'm afraid I can't accept the gift, however. You men really can't afford such a fine gift, and I really do prefer to walk."

Morgan was confused. "You like to walk?"

"Yes. I'm one of that rare breed that just likes to walk. If I have a horse, I need to take care of him as well as myself, and I prefer not to do that.

I thought you ought to know, though, that I walk because I want to — not because I can't ride. In the future, if you have a horse you aren't man enough to break, let me know. I'll be glad to top him off for you."

Morgan's face turned crimson and he opened his mouth to speak, but the grinning Sky Pilot had already turned and walked away, leaving Morgan holding the reins of the exhausted horse. The assembled hands roared with laughter and called out gleeful insults to Morgan. As they climbed down to follow the Sky Pilot to the house for dinner, Morgan swore and began to unsaddle the horse and rub him down.

When Morgan returned to the house the rest were already seated for dinner. As he entered several began to hurraw him.

"Hey, Morgan, the joke's on you this time."

"Guess what, Morgan. That Sky Pilot can ride circles around you."

"Why don't you preach and let him break your horses?"

"Sure nice of you to fix up that old saddle for the boss."

With a grin Morgan walked over to the Sky Pilot and stuck out his hand. "Rever'nd, you sure got the best of me on that one. That was one hell of a ride! I, I, uh, I mean, uh, that there was a mighty fine ride."

The Sky Pilot grinned and stood to shake his hand. "Thank you, Morgan. You picked a good horse. That was a much better ride than the one the boys over at the Gantz ranch fixed me up with last week."

5

"WELL, Keed, you think you be ready?"

Wayne grinned in response to Pete's question, with no premonition what the decision would mean before the summer was over. It had been several weeks of intense training, but he handled the dogs and the sheep well. "Ready as I'll ever be, I guess," he responded.

Pete nodded. "Tomorrow you take sheeps to Bald Knob bedground. Camp-jack he set your wagon for you."

The sun was about to appear over the mountains the next morning when Wayne whistled for his dogs. "Mickey! Runt!" he called. "Let's move 'em out."

He waved his hat to start them, then rode out, knowing the dogs would move the band of sheep to follow. He saw his sheep wagon already ahead of them. He addressed his horse. "Well, Streak, there goes home. By the time we get these woollies to the bedground, Art will have us set up and be waitin' for us."

He knew Art, the camp-jack, would leave him the next morning, but be back every three days to move the sheep wagon to a new location. Each morning Wayne would move the sheep to water at daybreak, then let them spread out in one direction to graze. Before sundown he would move them back to water, then into the bedground. A bedground was always selected for its ability to hold the band where the dogs could protect them. Coyotes, bears, and an occasional mountain lion would prey on them it they were not protected.

The second morning on a bedground the same procedure would be followed, but they would be started in a different direction to graze. The fourth morning in a camp they would be started in the direction camp would be moved. On the fourth day they would be watered and bedded down in a different bedground.

Each time the camp-jack made the rounds of his three herders he would return to the ranch. He would report their condition and activities and restock his own supply wagon. On smaller outfits the foreman was usually the camp-jack, but on bigger outfits like the Rocking R he had too many other things to supervise.

Wayne's first month on the mountains was almost idyllic. He began to wonder why anyone would ever leave such a life as this. At night he would lie in his bunk in the sheep wagon and think, "If a man just had a woman to share it with, this life would be perfect." Then with LaDonna's face smiling in his mind he would drift into sleep.

It wasn't until near the end of June he caught the first inkling of trouble. He wakened in his sheep wagon in the hour before daylight and lay listening a few moments. Assured everything was normal he rolled out and dressed. He started a fire in the wagon's stove and mixed a batch of biscuits. Breaking the film of ice in the water bucket, he made a pot of coffee. He fed the dogs and walked to the spring for a fresh bucket of water. As he walked back to the wagon, Runt let out a low growl. Wayne looked in the direction the dog was watching for several seconds before he spotted them.

"I see 'em, Runt."

The dog quieted. Two men rode out of a small stand of aspen about a half-mile below the bedground and stopped to look around.

"Spotted our smoke," he told the dog. "Looks like they're headin' up to talk."

He didn't know if he was just accustomed to being alone or felt some premonition, but he felt the hair on the back of his neck rising to match his dog's. As the men turned his direction he took the water into the wagon. He took the Dutch oven with the hot biscuits off the fire and picked up his thirty-thirty. Stepping outside he moved into the edge of the trees away from the wagon and waited.

As they rode up he noted the FX brand on the two horses and thought, "Fox's outfit. They're out of their territory quite a ways."

The two rode to about twenty feet from the sheep wagon, then spread about thirty feet apart to either side of it and faced the door. "Mornin' in the wagon," the taller of the two men called out.

Wayne stepped into sight about forty feet from them. His position allowed him to see them both in almost a straight line. If he had been in the wagon and come out its door he would have been unable to look at both of them at once. "Mornin'," he answered them. "Get down and come in. Got the coffee on. You fellas are just in time for breakfast."

The two were obviously uncomfortable with the surprise arrangement, and sat their horses nervously. The shorter of the two responded, "Guess we'll pass on the breakfast," he said. "Seems a little unneighbourly to eat a man's food then tell him he's gotta move out."

Wayne felt his stomach tighten. "Move out? Why would I want to move out?"

The tall one answered. "Fox is plannin' to move a couple bunches of cattle up this way. Them danged sheep eat the grass so close there ain't none left for cattle to graze on. Them sheep's gotta move out so's they can. He figures you can be gone inside of three days."

Wayne's jaw tightened. He used the end of his gun barrel to push his hat back, then merely lowered the barrel back against his shoulder, with his right hand holding the pistol grip. His finger was in the trigger guard, and he knew he could swing down and fire from that position much faster than most cowboys could draw and shoot a pistol. He knew they knew it as well.

"This is government range," he reminded them. "Lessman's used it quite a few years, and we was on it first this year. You tell Fox if he sends cattle to range I'm herdin' on they won't stop runnin' till they cross Powder River."

The tall man leaned forward and rested a forearm across his saddle horn and pushed his hat back on his head. He scratched his ear. "You're sure makin' a mistake, Kid," he said. "You might be pretty salty but you can't stand up to the likes of the men Fox is hirin'. You don't leave he'll probably send Davis up after you, and they'll take you off the mountain in a pine box."

"Who's Davis? I never heard of him."

"You try to stick around here and you will. They call him 'Coyote Davis', and he's just about like a coyote in these mountains. They tell me a man just don't see him till it's too late. You take my advice, Kid, you'll pick up your time and quit the country."

With no further words the two wheeled their horses and left the clearing at a fast trot. Wayne stood watching them until they were out of sight.

"Well, Runt," he told his dogs, "looks like we're in for a fight."

The sheep were restless to leave the bedground, and Mickey was having all he could do to hold them. Wayne looked toward the breakfast and hot coffee waiting in the sheep wagon, then looked again at the sheep. He signalled for the dogs to take them to water.

"Guess I'll eat cold biscuits today," he mumbled to himself. "At least I can heat the coffee back up."

He followed the sheep, cradling his thirty-thirty in the crook of his arm. When they had drunk their fill and began grazing he left the dogs to batch them and returned to the sheep wagon. He ate a cold breakfast but didn't really taste it. His mind was too much on things to come.

The sheep were the problem. If he got involved in any kind of running fight with the Fox outfit, the sheep would scatter all over the mountain. Without him, the dogs wouldn't know where to bed them down or what direction to move them. They would try to keep them bunched and stay with them, but they wouldn't be able to for long. The band of sheep would soon scatter into small bunches that would be easy prey for the predators.

The sheep also made him an easy target. He was restricted to staying with them, so he was easily found. His movements were regulated by the routine of those sheep, so anyone would know when he would be at water or at the wagon. He couldn't run. He couldn't hide. He couldn't even guess who or how many they would send against him.

He fixed up his bedroll and put some food and extra ammunition in it. He filled his canteen from the water bucket and saddled his horse. He tied the bedroll behind the saddle and hung the canteen on the saddle-horn. Then he went back inside and strapped on the New Service Colt forty-five. He tore off a corner of a newspaper the camp-jack had left and wrote him a note on it:

'Art,' it said, 'trouble with the Fox outfit. I'm hiding out away from my wagon till I see what they do. I'll sneak in for supplies and I'll keep the sheep OK. Keep moving me like always.'

He started to sign it 'Wayne', then thought better of it. "You know," he said out loud, "I ain't never been called 'Wayne' since I been here, 'cept by LaDonna." He signed the note 'Kid', looked at it for a moment, then added the name 'Hailer' behind it.

'Kid Hailer,' he said to himself. 'Sounds like somebody outa one of them dime novels.'

He left the note on the table, held down by a can of baking powder.

He rode back into the timber above the sheep wagon and began to circle toward where the dogs were watching the sheep. His eyes moved constantly across every bit of cover and back along his backtrail.

"It's too quick for 'em to be after me yet, Streak," he informed his horse, "but I'd best get in the habit of watching."

He followed the side of the ridge where he wouldn't be outlined against the sky. He took advantage of the edges of the timber, where he could see around without himself being easy to spot. He knew herding sheep had just become a whole different game, but he was ready for it. At least he thought he was.

It was three weeks later when the game became serious. Wayne had been keeping to the timber in sight of his sheep, and had seen nothing out of the ordinary, but he knew trouble would come, and he constantly imagined being shot at from every conceivable cover to keep his senses alert.

When he wanted to give his dogs instruction, he would position himself where they could see him, and whistle. When they looked toward the whistle he would hat-signal his instruction, then quickly duck into the brush or timber and move one way or another. At night, when the sheep were bedded down, he would scout the area around his wagon thoroughly, then slip in and feed his dogs and renew his supplies. He would then find a place away from the wagon to roll out his bedroll and sleep, but never twice in the same spot.

He didn't usually picket his horse. He carried a pair of hobbles in his saddle-bags. At night he hobbled the horse's front feet together. That allowed the horse to move around to better grass or water, but since he had to move both front feet together he wouldn't go far. In that way he was always close and easy to catch.

Each morning he packed his bedroll

and saddled his horse before daylight. He would again scout carefully around his sheep wagon, then slip in to tell his dogs to move the sheep to water.

It was in that morning scouting circle he found the sign. It was just a portion of a horse's track, but he knew at once it was not made by his horse. When he failed to find any other sign he sat his saddle in the timber a long while thinking. Filled with a sudden inspiration he slipped into his sheep wagon from the back side and slid under the canvas from the side away from the door. He built a fire in the cook stove, being sure there was some wood green enough to smoke. Then he slid back out the way he had come in and took up a position about thirty yards from the wagon, in a well-concealed position. The spot he chose was a thick clump of brush backed up against a cut bank where he knew nobody could come up behind him. He settled down to wait.

He had waited over an hour before

he saw his horse's ears perk up and his head come around. He held a hand across the horse's nose to keep him quiet, and waited. Across the clearing he caught a glimpse of movement in the brush facing the door of the wagon. A few minutes later a man stepped out of the brush holding a pistol in his hand. He crossed quickly to the wagon and stopped beside the door listening. Then he jerked the door open and swept the pistol across the interior, making sure it was empty. He looked around the clearing again, and, seeing nothing, put his pistol back in its holster. He pulled a glove from his back pocket and put it on.

The glove puzzled Wayne. The air was sharp and cold in the mornings, making a glove practical, but he had never heard of a gunman wearing gloves, at least on his right hand. He stepped out of the brush, holding his thirty-thirty cradled across the crook of his left arm, and called out. "You lookin' for me?"

The man whirled toward him, keeping both hands carefully in sight, away from his body. He looked Wayne over for nearly half a minute before answering. "You must be Kid Hailer," he said finally.

Wayne nodded. "They call me that."

"The boss said you'd been told to clear out."

"They said somethin' about that, all right. I told them it'd be one awful cold day in July when they run me off government range."

"Well, I'll tell you, Kid, it does get awful cold in July in this country. I broke ice for water many a time in July. You shoulda took their advice. Now I gotta run you off."

Wayne felt an icy chill at the cool way the man said it. He asked, "Are you Davis?"

There was a flicker in his eyes, but Davis didn't move. "Uh huh. You going to leave or do I have to kill you?"

Wayne was still puzzled by the gloves,

but he had watched as Davis talked and noted that he had brought his hands together in front of him. As he watched he saw the fingers of Davis's left hand tighten on the finger tips of the right glove. He reacted. He whipped the end of the rifle barrel up to cover Davis and yelled, "Hold it!"

Davis froze. He had slid his right hand out of the glove and grabbed his pistol in one smooth motion that Wayne hadn't even seen. He was holding his pistol half way out of the holster. Blood was pounding in Wayne's temples and his stomach felt hollow.

'He's fast!' he thought. 'If I hadn't seen his fingers tighten on the glove he'd have drawn and shot me before I could move!'

Sharply he said, "Put it back and move your hand away from it."

Davis continued to hold his pistol and weigh his chances for several seconds, then he slowly opened his hand and lowered the pistol back into its holster. He put the glove that was still dangling from his left hand on. Still looking at Wayne he said, "It's a hell of a note when a man'll get himself killed over something that ain't even his!"

Ignoring Wayne then he turned his back and walked away into the brush. He rode out on his horse a minute later and rode from sight away from the clearing. Wayne kept the gun trained on him until he was out of sight, then walked over and sat down on the steps of his sheep wagon. His knees had begun trembling violently. The colour washed out of his face, and he sat there on the rock staring into nothing.

"That's as close to dead as I want to get!" he said to nobody in particular.

When he had sat there for several minutes the colour came back into his face. He stood up and said aloud, "Well, I can't sit around here thinking how close that one was. I better find my sheep and check on them."

He walked back to where he had left his horse, slid his rifle into the scabbard, and rode after the sheep. He had ridden about half a mile when a new thought struck him, and he reined in abruptly.

"Wait a minute!" he said. "That man is Coyote Davis. He didn't get that name for nothin'. He snuck up on my wagon to shoot me from the brush. Sure's anything he'll be layin' for me somewhere."

He sat there thinking about it for a minute. He had to check those sheep. That was his job. The only thing he could do was try to be ready. He drew the rifle out of its scabbard and checked to be sure there was a shell in the chamber. He cocked the hammer and laid it across the saddle in front of him, holding the reins in his left hand and the pistol grip of the rifle in his right. He rode slowly, watching every possible cover for movement, watching the birds to see any indication of a hidden intruder. Every nerve was taut as a bowstring.

He had ridden nearly a mile when a sound in the brush to his left caused him to whip his rifle around. A cottontail rabbit crashed out of the brush and into a hole under a rock. He looked back quickly, trying to see what had scared the rabbit, but saw and heard nothing. He started to ride on.

When he saw his horse's ears go forward and his head turn toward a clump of brush, Wayne was already moving in a long dive to the ground. He heard the bark of a rifle as he hit the ground, and he rolled his feet under him and jumped behind a tree. A bullet tore bark from the edge of the tree as he stood up, and he turned sideways to be sure no target extended beyond the tree's cover.

He looked around deliberately. To his right a shallow draw extended at an angle, with the bank marked by rocks and brush. If he could dive into that draw he would have the advantage of being able to pick his own vantage-point. Here, he was pinned down, and couldn't get into a position to shoot without exposing himself. He took his hat off and threw it to his left at the same instant he made a dive to his right. He had no illusion that Davis was green enough to shoot at the hat, but he hoped it would distract him enough to make him miss the real target. It worked.

As he hit the ground beyond the edge of the wash he realized it was deeper than he thought. He hit the ground hard and the wind was knocked from his lungs. Gripping his rifle he scrambled to a position behind a clump of greasewood and fought to catch his breath.

When his breathing returned to normal he eased along the edge of the wash to a spot about thirty feet from where he had entered. He slowly extended his head up behind a clump of wild rose bush. He studied the brush the shots had come from, but saw nothing. It was a waiting game now, to see who would move first.

He dropped back below the rim of the wash and considered the situation.

Davis could wait for him to move, or leave and wait for a better time. The next time he might not be so lucky. If there was a way to make him show himself now, it would save a lot of danger later. But how?

He found a stick about four feet long. He took off his neckerchief and wrapped it around a wad of small branches to make a round shape about the size of his head. Then he rubbed the neckerchief in the dirt and attached it to the stick.

Easing back to the bush he had been behind, he placed the stick across a rock about two feet to his left, with a tall cluster of grass on the rim of the wash in front of it. He brought his rifle to bear on the spot he thought Davis was hiding, then stepped on the short end of the stick. The force of stepping on that end of the stick caused the other end, with the neckerchief attached, to swing up and across, behind the clump of tall grass. As it did a bullet tore a hole in it. Wayne spotted the tiny puff of smoke in the brush and fired at it, then as quickly as he could lever his rifle, he shot about two feet to both sides of the spot.

One of the shots was followed by the unmistakable 'thwack' of a bullet striking flesh. There was a crash of something falling into brush, then silence. Wayne waited for five minutes that seemed like an hour without moving, but he heard no further sound. Then, cautiously, he lifted his head further to look around. There was no movement.

He retrieved his neckerchief from the stick and looked at the hole in it. That queasy feeling returned to his stomach. It made him tremble to realize the man he was pitted against was quick enough and good enough to shoot at a fleeting glimpse of something that size, and hit it dead centre! He untied it, shook the brush and dirt from it, and put it back on.

He moved a hundred yards down the

draw before climbing out. He stood silent and still, trying to detect sound or movement. He found neither. He walked back to retrieve his hat and put it on, then circled to the brush from which the shots had come. With his rifle ready he stepped softly toward the spot he knew Davis must be.

Stepping around a boulder he saw him. As he stepped into sight Davis fired and Wayne returned the fire so quickly the two shots sounded almost as one. Wayne felt a searing burn across the side of his head as Davis dropped his pistol and fell back. He levered another shell into the chamber and waited, but he did not move.

Warily, Wayne walked to him and kicked the pistol out of reach. He stopped to be certain the man was dead. He had two bullet holes in his chest. The first had hit a lung, but had not immediately killed him. He had waited silently, determined to live long enough to take Wayne with him. The second bullet had hit his heart, and he died instantly.

Wayne stood up and felt dizzy. He put a hand to his head and it came away covered with blood. His exploring fingers found the top half of his left ear gone, and it was bleeding down across his shoulder. He said to himself, 'Now what do I do? If I tie this dirty neckerchief around it, it'll get infected. If I don't, it'll bleed all over everything.'

He shook the neckerchief out again and tied it tightly around his head to stop the bleeding. He checked Davis's pockets. He had a couple gold coins and some paper money, a plug of Red Man Chewing Tobacco, and nothing more. He removed his gunbelt, put the pistol back in the holster and wrapped the belt around it, and laid it aside. Then he dragged Davis to the wash and caved dirt off the bank to bury him.

He worked back and forth through the trees behind where Davis had hidden until he found his horse. He put Davis's rifle in the saddle scabbard, noting there was quite a bit of blood on it. He tied a knot in the reins and looped them over the saddle-horn, then slapped the horse on the rump. He ran off aways, looked back, then started walking. It was wearing an FX brand, and Wayne knew it would go home.

He walked back to his own horse. He put his rifle in the scabbard and put Davis's rolled-up gunbelt in his saddle-bag. "Well, Streak," he addressed his horse, "we better get a move on if we're gonna get those sheep to the bedground by dark."

When he got to the sheep wagon the camp-jack was there. He called out, "'Bout time you got here, Kid. I came in tonight so's we could get a jump on movin' you tomorrow. What happened to your head?"

"Glad to see you, Art. I got an ear shot off."

"Shot off? Who shot at you?"

"Coyote Davis. He won't be sneak-shootin' anyone else though. I killed him."

"You killed Coyote Davis? Well I'll be danged. He's killed a dozen men or more. Some say upwards of eighteen or twenty."

"I can believe it. He was better and faster than anyone I've seen."

"Well, come on, Kid, let's heat up some water and take care of that head. Just your ear, you say?"

"I think so. That's all I could feel."

They went into the sheep wagon and Art put water on to heat. He went to his supply wagon and returned with a clean flour sack. When the water was hot he cleaned the wound carefully and got the rest of the blood cleaned off Wayne's head.

"Looks like he nicked your head just a dab," he observed. "Nothin' to worry about. We'll fix 'er up good as new."

Art took a big cud of tobacco out of his mouth and laid it on a strip of the flour sacking. Wayne asked, "What are you doing with the tobacco?"

"Gonna put it on your ear. Chewin' tobacco's the best poultice there is.

109

Hadn't oughta never bandage a wound or fix a snake bite without it."

He wrapped the cloth around Wayne's head so the cud of tobacco was held against the wound, and tied it tightly. "Kinda hard to tie without blindfoldin' you, but I guess that'll do. What are you going to do now?"

"I'm going to herd sheep like I was hired to do," Wayne replied. "I sent Davis's horse home. Maybe they'll figure out they don't want to mess with me and back off."

Art looked dubious. "They might, but I wouldn't count on it. You watch yourself real close. They might just send someone else."

The next morning Wayne moved out with his sheep and Art moved the wagon to a new bedground and left. As soon as he was out of sight, Wayne unbandaged his head, got rid of the tobacco, then wrapped it up again.

"Danged if I want that stuff on my head," he muttered.

6

WAYNE approached his sheep wagon every evening with a tightness in his stomach and every sense alert. He seldom slept in it, using it as a base but reluctant to let himself be trapped in it. Days turned into weeks, however, with no further incidents. He had almost decided he was right in thinking the Fox outfit would back off now, when more trouble came.

Wayne had just bedded the sheep down for the night. He circled the sheep wagon, keeping in the brush out of sight, watching for sign of any intruder. He was ready to step into the open when he heard soft footfalls of a slowly walking horse. He crouched and waited.

"Keed?" He recognized Pete's voice at once. "Are you in camp?"

Wayne stepped out of the brush and Pete's horse shied at the suddenness of his appearance. "Pete!" he exclaimed, "you're a sight for sore eyes! How are you?"

"Not good, Keed. You are in trouble. I ride to warn you."

"Warn me? What's the problem?"

"The sheriff, he came clear from Casper for you. He say you are stealing the sheeps of Mr. Lessman."

The colour drained from Wayne's face. The world retreated to a faint and far-away place, leaving only him and Pete standing in a swirl of impossibility.

"What?! Me, stealing sheep? How could I do that? What could I do with them? That's crazy! I ain't left the mountain all summer."

Pete nodded. "I know, Keed. I know you are honest. I know you would not steal from your own outfit, but they have evidence. The sheriff he comes with others to arrest you and take you back to Casper to put you in jail there."

Wayne studied Pete's face for a long moment. He turned a little away and looked off across the country where the sun was sinking behind the Wind River Mountains in the distance. He stood there without moving for several minutes, then turned to Pete.

"I guess they'll just have to do that, then. There can't be very good proof for something I didn't do, so I'll just go along with them. I sure ain't going to fight the law."

Pete shook his head. "No, *amigo*, you must not go with them. You must not be here when they come. I think if they find you, you will not live to get to the jail. They will kill you."

"It just don't make sense, Pete. What have they got for proof?"

"They have sheep hides. A homesteader from over on Horse Creek was caught with the hides of Mr. Lessman's sheep. He tell that you are giving him the sheeps for half the money he gets."

Wayne was stunned. "Why would he

say that? Who is he?"

"I think he is somebody that Fox has made to say these things. He is afraid to come any more after you, so he has found the way to get the sheriff to do that for him. He has sent two mens for you, and they have not come back."

"What good's it going to do him to get the sheriff after me?"

"There are mens with the sheriff that I think are working for Fox. They will try to get the sheriff to hang you, or they will shoot you and say you try to run. You must not be here."

"I suppose you're right, but it galls me sore to run from something I ain't done. Pete, if I run now, how am I ever going to clear my name?"

"I do not know, *amigo*, but I know you cannot clear your name when you are dead. You must go."

"You going to take care of my sheep?"

"*Si*. I will stay with them until Curt get a different herder to come."

Wayne looked across the darkening

country again, studying the spot behind which the sun had sunk. "OK. I'll fix a sack of grub and get my bedroll."

Pete followed and they talked as he worked. He rolled his bedroll and took all the extra ammunition he had. He left his own forty-five strapped on, but took the one he had taken from Davis as well. He tied the bedroll behind his saddle, packed the other things into the saddlebags, and took time to give the horse a double handful of oats.

The horse lapped the oats greedily, but was still obviously impatient at not being unsaddled. He had already had a long day, and looked longingly at the lush grass. "Sorry, Streak," Wayne told him. "I know you're ready to eat and rest, but looks like we gotta go."

He mounted and turned back to Pete. "Pete, you tell Mr. Lessman what I told you. Tell him I'd sure like to think I'm still working for him. I'll find a way to prove I'm innocent as soon as I can."

He started to ride away, then stopped

and turned back. "Pete, would you be sure to tell LaDonna I ain't never stole anything from anyone, especially the outfit I work for. I want her to know that."

"*Si*. I will tell her. *Adios, amigo. Vaya con Dios*."

"What's that mean?"

"It means, 'Go with God', my friend."

"Uh, thanks, Pete."

Without waiting for an answer he turned his horse and rode off into the deepening night. "Streak, I ain't sure where we're goin'," he muttered to his horse, "but we better put some distance between us and camp. I'spect we better head up over the top and see what's on the east slope."

He rode in anger for a while, until the anger gave way to resentment, then fear, then he was buried under an avalanche of self-pity. Why did all this happen to him? He lost his father, then his home, then his whole circle of friends. Then, just when it looked

116

like he was finding a new life to settle into, he lost that too, and with it his reputation. Twice now he had nearly lost his life.

He pounded the pommel of his saddle with the side of his fist. "I'll show 'em!" he gritted between his teeth. "I'll show 'em all. They'll find out what it is to mess with Wayne Hill!"

The absurdity of his actions struck him and he blushed, but this time there was nobody to see. "Now, how am I goin' to do that?" he asked aloud. "I don't know anybody off the Rocking R. I don't know the country off of this range. I don't know the guy that lied about me. I wouldn't even know him if I saw him! I don't even dare show my face to ask any questions. I can't even go back to collect my wages!"

He considered the possibility of riding clear out of the country. "What is it back home — maybe two hundred fifty miles? I could be there in two weeks. Once I get out of Natrona

County they ain't apt to even be looking for me."

The thought seemed good until he considered it longer. Then he knew he couldn't do it. He wasn't going to turn tail and run and leave the name of a thief behind! He rode on with LaDonna's face always in the front of his mind.

"I wonder if she believes I'm a thief?"

Before midnight it began to rain. He untied his slicker from his saddle, unrolled it, and put it on. He pulled the wide-brimmed Stetson down over his face, and winced as it touched his still-tender half-ear. He slouched in the saddle and rode into the night, always bearing north-east and climbing.

When the sky began to lighten toward dawn he started looking for a place to hole up. He stopped twice at small streams to let his horse drink and grab a few mouthfuls of grass. While he did, he climbed ridges to look over the country, but found nothing that looked like what he needed. About midday he made a pot of coffee over a small fire and ate some biscuits and dried mutton, then went on.

Late in the afternoon he topped out on a ridge and spotted a wisp of smoke from the far side of a deep canyon. He rode into the canyon slowly and watchfully. When he had crossed a good-sized stream in the bottom he saw a cabin nestled into a corner against the north wall of the canyon. There was smoke coming from the chimney. He rode to the edge of the clearing and sat his horse while he looked around.

"Hello, the house," he called.

The answer came at once. "Hello yourself! Get down and come in!"

Wayne dropped to the ground and left his horse standing with the reins on the ground as he approached the door. He knew the horse would stand there until severe hunger or thirst forced him to move.

The cabin door was open and a big man stepped into it. His head brushed the top of the door frame and his shoulders nearly touched both sides. He wore buckskin trousers over long underwear, but no shirt. He had a full beard and long hair. His boots looked like he had made them himself of bear skin. He might have been anywhere between thirty-five and sixty, and looked like he could have killed a bear with a willow switch.

He grinned, showing a mouth with less than half enough teeth to fill it. "Better put your horse over there where he can get somethin' to eat and drink, kid, then come on in and have a bite."

Wayne stopped and looked back at his horse. It was obvious the horse was going no further without food and rest. He said, "Well, I'd sure be obliged for something for my horse, but a cup of coffee is all I need."

The big man's grin widened. "Aw, you'd eat a bite too if it was good and clean, wouldn't you?"

The smell of smoked meat cooking

was making his mouth water and stomach growl. Wayne said, "Well, yeah, I could use a bite to eat. I been riding a while."

He hobbled his horse near an area of good grass close to the creek. He carried the saddle to the corral and hung it across the top rail, hanging the bridle from the saddle-horn. Then he walked into the cabin, staggering slightly.

The cabin was clean and neat as a pin. The bunk against the back wall was made up. There were wooden pegs all around the walls with things hanging in place. Except for the absence of rugs and curtains, it looked like a woman's hand was involved in its care.

Seeing a trapper's cabin like that took Wayne by surprise, and he just stood there, staring around. Watching his surprise, the trapper chuckled. "Look like home, Kid?"

"Uh, yeah, uh, it don't look like most trappers' cabins."

"Well, I figure bein' alone don't

mean I gotta be dirty. After my wife's death I swore I wasn't never gonna get like most bachelors in this country."

Wayne's surprise showed. "You had a wife? Here?"

The trapper's eyes clouded. "Not here. 'Nother place. Come and eat. Gettin' cold."

Wayne sat up to the table and filled his plate with smoked meat and fried potatoes, biscuits, and stewed raisins. "I haven't seen raisins for a long time," Wayne said. "What's this meat? It's a lot like bacon, but it's different."

"It's bacon all right," the trapper responded, "but it never seen no hog. It's bear bacon. I decided a bear's just as fat as a hog in the fall, and a fella oughta be able to slice that belly fat just like they do with hogs and smoke it. I got me a little smoke house out back, and by gol it works purty good."

Wayne helped himself to seconds and they ate with no further conversation until the meal was done. When they had finished, the trapper walked over to a shelf by the stove and took down a long-stemmed pipe, filled it from a small crock, and pulled a coal from the fire to light it. When he had it going well he set his chair outside, just beside the door, and leaned back against the cabin wall. Wayne followed the example and sat on the other side of the door. They sat there in silence for several minutes, until the trapper broke it.

"My name's Charlie Taylor, kid. Wanta tell me yours?"

Wayne's chair came back down on all four legs with a bang. He sat ramrod straight, looking at the trapper with his eyes wide. "Charlie Taylor?"

"You look like you seen a ghost, kid. That name mean somethin' to you?"

Wayne felt his face turn red. "Well, yes. No! Well, I guess it couldn't be you or nothin'. It's just that my dad used to talk about an old friend of his by that name a lot, and . . ."

Charlie watched his stammering confusion through the smoke of his pipe for quite a while before answering. "Well now, you surely favour a man I used to know years ago," he said finally. "Could be, I s'pose. Your dad wouldn't be Levi Hill by chance?"

Wayne sat in stunned silence. He knew he must have looked stupid, sitting there with his mouth opening and shutting like a fish without water, swallowing like he had a mouthful he couldn't get down, and saying nothing. When he could command his voice he croaked, "You knew my dad?"

"Yessir, I did that, if Levi is your dad."

"Yeah, he's my dad."

"Finest man I ever knew." Charlie looked Wayne up and down. "Your dad was hell on wheels in a fight. Last I knew he lit out and went back east somewheres, runnin' from a murder charge for killin' a man he didn't kill. Fella that did the killin' got found out, but nobody knowed where Levi was by then. But enough of that. Where's Levi at?"

Wayne knew his eyes filled with tears, but he couldn't help it. Blinking furiously to fight them back he said, "He's dead. Died of pneumonia couple winters ago."

Then, without really meaning to, Wayne poured out his whole story, ending with his arrival here at the cabin this afternoon. Charlie listened in silence, puffing his pipe and looking across the country until Wayne had finished. Into the silence that followed his story, Charlie said softly, "What now, Kid?"

Wayne shrugged. "I guess I don't know. I want to clear my name somehow, and stop Fox from running Lessman out of business, but I guess I don't have any notion how to go about it."

Charlie considered it for a while before he spoke again. "Well, unless I miss my guess they won't do nothin' much no more this year. Sounds like you put a real kink in their plans there. They got to start moving down lower on the mountains 'fore the middle of September, and it's August a'ready."

Wayne nodded. "Yeah, I s'pose. But next spring it'll start all over."

"Could be. What say you winter here with me? You help me with my trap line, and we'll spend some time figgerin'. Come spring we'll drop over there and maybe see what we can do. Might be they won't be expectin' you by then."

Wayne thought about it quite a while. He didn't like the idea a bit of sitting here all winter with everyone thinking he was a thief, but he didn't know any other answers either. Finally he said, "Well, OK, if you want me to."

"You ever do any trappin'?"

"Little, along the White River back home. It ain't much of a river . . . just a crick. Mostly trapped skunks and 'coon and fox."

"This's different than that, but you'll learn."

"Uh huh. Guess it'll sure beat tryin'

to hole up all winter by myself."

Charlie got up. "Just as well throw your stuff in the cabin. You can sleep on the floor tonight. Tomorrow we'll peel some poles and make you a bunk."

The following days and weeks were busy as Wayne and Charlie prepared for the trapping season, got the hide shack rodent-tight, stacked hay for winter feed for the horses, and built a huge woodstack for fuel. In the evenings they talked, and Wayne learned more about his father's early life than he had ever known.

One evening as they talked, Wayne brought up the subject again. "What did they do to the guy that really killed the one Dad got blamed for?" he asked.

"They hung him over at Buffalo. Just hung him from the sign in front of Thompson's General Store. Terrible thing to watch a man die like that, even a killer. They just hauled on the rope till they lifted his feet off the ground, and he kicked and twisted like everything. His eyes bugged way out and he turned all purple-like afore he finally died. I rode twenty miles through mud and rain to watch 'em hang that man, just cause he got Levi blamed for what he done. I wouldn't walk across the street to watch 'em hang another one! I tell you, I saw that man dancin' on the end o' that rope every time I went to sleep for a month, an' him deservin' to hang if ever a man did."

Another evening they fell to discussion of Wayne's pistol.

"Can't figure Levi lettin' you use a sidearm like that there," Charlie offered, nodding at that New Service Colt forty-five.

"What's wrong with it?" Wayne asked. "It's dependable and shoots straight."

"Reckon so," Charlie agreed, "but it ain't made for drawin' atall."

"How come?"

"Grip's too big. Frame's too heavy. Action's too slow."

"Well," Wayne offered, "Dad never would teach me to draw fast anyway."

"That figures," Charlie said. "Your pa never thought a fast draw was important, even though he was about as fast as I ever seen."

"My dad was?"

"He sure was, but he never relied on it. I 'spect that's why he wouldn't teach you. Didn't want you relyin' on it neither."

"I'd still like to learn."

"If you had a gun made for it, I'd teach you."

Wayne got up and went to his bunk. From beneath he pulled a small bundle and unwrapped it. He took out the gun and holster he had taken from Davis and handed it to Charlie.

Charlie took it with a low whistle. "Now that's a different weapon completely. This is a gun-fighter's weapon. It's a Colt forty-five, but notice how different the frame is? It's got a smaller grip, lighter weight, and the front sight's been filed off so it won't hang up in the holster. Where'd you get it?"

"I took it off Coyote Davis after I shot him," Wayne explained.

"Well, that's the hard way to get one, but you got yourself one fine weapon. Strap it on, so we can see where it's comfortable."

Wayne swung it around his hips after he removed his other one, and they adjusted the belt to the right size.

"You want it to hang where you can reach it easy," Charlie lectured, "but not too low. If it's too low it gets in the way of walkin' and workin' and everythin' else. The big thing is to have it where it feels natural for you to grab it, and where it's at a comfortable height for you to shoot when you get it drawn."

They talked a while longer and went to bed. The next morning they opened the door to a world made clean by six inches of new snow. The air carried a sharp bite of cold that promised things to come. It felt so clean and tangy in his lungs Wayne wanted to stand there and breathe the whole mountain into himself. The world was so clean, so white, so perfect he wanted to stand there and study it, absorb it, breathe it in until the stillness settled within and became a part of him.

The spell was broken by Charlie's words. "Soon's we eat a bite we'll get the traps lined out and set. It's time to go to work."

They ate quickly. Carrying all the traps they could handle they started upstream, setting them carefully in the most likely places, covering their scent and their tracks, then moving on. By midday they had set upstream as far as their traps would reach, and returned. Loading up again they did the same downstream. By the time the entire trap-line was in place and they had returned to the cabin, it was dark.

When they had eaten and cleaned up, Wayne started to drop into bed. Charlie stopped him. "I know you're tired, Kid, but if you intend to be fast with that gun you got to practise every day, not just when you feel like it. You make sure you don't never draw it less than a hundred times a day, every day, no matter how tired you are nor how bad you feel. You count 'em. One hundred times. Everyday."

With a sigh Wayne strapped on the gun, checked to make sure the cylinder was empty, and practised drawing it the designated one hundred times. Then he collapsed into bed.

It was still dark when Charlie shook him awake. "Roll out, Kid. Most stuff we trap will be caught in the night. I don't like to leave 'em there to suffer. You take upstream and I'll take down."

The winter fell into a routine. Early check of the trap-line, take care of the hides, listen to Charlie lecture on this and that, and practise his quick draw. The first week he was amazed at the soreness of his arm muscles, but they conditioned quickly. Charlie showed him how to thumb the hammer as he drew, so there was no time lapse between drawing and firing. He corrected each bad habit he saw start to develop, and kept making little suggestions to improve either the smoothness of the draw or the accuracy of the shooting. He taught him how important it was to have his feet placed properly, to watch the angle of the sun, and to allow for shooting uphill or down, until it all became second nature.

It was a busy winter filled with hard work, but Wayne enjoyed it. There were times when they would have much rather not put on coats and snowshoes to check the traps in the middle of fierce storms, but neither could stand the thought of animals trapped and slowly freezing to death, so they always went out.

Storm or sunshine, no day went by without Wayne practising at least a hundred times the drawing and shooting of his gun. The callous the hammer wore on his thumb thickened until it no longer hurt. The action of drawing and firing became so natural it needed neither thought nor concentration.

Charlie usually practised with him, and began to regain much of his own speed. Wayne at first was certain he had never seen anything move with the speed of Charlie's draw, but Charlie said, "You're goin' to be faster than I ever was, Kid. You got a natural knack for it."

Before spring the truth of his words was evident. He was no longer any match for Wayne. In daylight Wayne dreamed of clearing his name and setting things right for the Lessmans' Rocking R. At night he dreamed of only one of the Lessmans.

7

THE winter was endless for LaDonna. When the sheriff had come from Casper with three cars filled with men, she had listened, stunned, to the things they had to say. She had seen Pete saddle a horse and ride out, keeping the barn between himself and the men until well out of sight, so she knew Wayne would be warned. She watched her father carefully for any sign that he believed the charges brought against Wayne, and was satisfied he did not. She hadn't either. Not then.

All winter, however, new accusations had drifted into the ranch. Some said that Wayne was really an escaped prisoner from New Mexico, or a gunman from Montana, or a kid that had killed his whole family in Colorado and was on the run. Some said he was a notorious killer that had shot twelve or fourteen men, most of them in cold blood.

As the rumours and speculation continued to mount she began to have doubts. She brought up the subject to her mother. "Do you think Wayne really stole our sheep?"

Her mother looked at her carefully. "You don't, do you?"

"No! I mean, I don't think he would. But if he's as green as he was supposed to be, why did he move so quickly when Dad was shot?"

Her mother nodded. "I've thought of that. He's either been shot at before or had some awfully good training."

LaDonna instantly became defensive. "He said his father had taught him things like that since he was little. He said he got sick when he shot him because he'd never killed anyone before."

Marion Lessman smiled. "Then why don't you believe him?"

LaDonna raised her hands and

dropped them to her sides. "I don't know! It's just that . . . well, how did he manage to kill Coyote Davis? He was a professional killer and he was supposed to be hunting Wayne. And if he was innocent, why did he run?"

"Didn't you say Pete warned him and told him to run until it could be cleared up?"

"Yes, I know, Mother. But why would a squatter on Fox's land lie?"

"I think you know the answer to that, LaDonna. If Fox offered to let him stay and homestead there in exchange for a lie, that man would say anything. I think Fox made up the whole thing just to get rid of Wayne. I think he's really afraid of him."

LaDonna's doubts battled constantly with her memories of Wayne's face as they had talked. "Mother, his face is just so — I don't know — so — open. I just can't believe he's anything other that what he says. I don't think he could lie if he wanted to!"

Marion smiled again. "Not without

blushing anyway. That boy blushes more than anyone I ever knew."

LaDonna giggled. "I know it. It embarrasses me sometimes just to see him so embarrassed. Then I tease him just to make him blush some more."

"You really like him, don't you?"

Now it was LaDonna's turn to blush. "I like him enough to be pretty sure he's no thief and no killer," she acknowledged.

The winter dragged by with no word from him or about him. It was as though he had dropped off the edge of the earth. She helped her mother with the book-keeping for the ranch, so she knew her father was still sending half of Wayne's wages to his mother each month, as though he was still working for the outfit, but the letters that came to him remained stacked on the desk, unopened and unanswered.

Pondering it one afternoon she was startled from her reverie by the dogs barking. As she looked out the window she saw a stranger ride into the yard. He was riding a tall sorrel and white pinto horse. It looked shaggy with its long winter coat, but was obviously strong, well-fed, and well-cared for. The rider was a big man, maybe an inch over six feet, broad shouldered, with a reddish complexion. He wore the usual high-crowned wide-brimmed Stetson of Wyoming, a sheepskin-lined coat with the collar turned up around his ears. He rode with his head scrunched down into his collar so that his hatbrim seemed to rest on it, shutting the cold wind from the back of his neck. He wore two neckerchieves instead of one, providing a little extra protection from the cold. He carried a Winchester thirty-thirty in a saddle scabbard under his left stirrup, with the butt forward. Something about him reminded her a little of Wayne, and she caught her breath as he rode up to the house.

Lessman stepped out onto the porch. "Get down and come in," he called.

"Thanks," the stranger answered. "Don't mind if I do. Mind if I put my horse in the barn and give him a bait of oats first?"

"Go right ahead," Lessman answered. "Stick him in any stall that's empty. Supper'll be ready pretty quick. We'll put a plate on."

"Much obliged." The stranger walked to the barn, leading his horse. By the time he returned the hands were in the crew's dining-room for supper. He joined the crew where the extra plate was set and fell to eating with no more than a nod of greeting to the crew.

When they had all finished eating, some of the hands lingered for a few minutes, obviously wanting the stranger to join in the conversations so they could find out about him, but he simply listened in silence, giving careful attention to everything said, but making no response. When all the crew had gone and the cook was clearing the table, he stepped to the door leading into the rest of the house and knocked on the jamb of the open door.

From the sitting-room Lessman called, "Come on in."

Hat in hand, the stranger entered. "Mr. Lessman?"

"Uh huh."

"I want to thank you for the supper and the keep for my horse. My name's Ray Wolverton. I wonder if I might talk to you for a little bit?"

Lessman hesitated. "What about?"

"You got a kid working for you by the name of Wayne Hill?"

Both LaDonna and her mother were sitting across the room. LaDonna gave a small gasp at the mention of Wayne's name, her hand flying to her mouth and her eyes widening.

Lessman's answer was evasive. "Had a kid by that name last summer. What's your interest in him?"

Wolverton looked at the three of them carefully in turn. Then, as though he had satisfied himself about something, he gave a barely perceptible nod and began to explain.

"I guess you need to know who I

am. I homestead up on Willow Creek. I been hearin' some stuff about this kid that works for you, but didn't pay no mind. Then I got this letter from my sister sayin' she sorta lost track of her son when he come to work for you, and could I maybe check on him."

Lessman looked thoughtful. "That'd be your nephew."

"Yup. She said she gets twenty dollars from him every month, but never no letter or nothin' with it. She says that just ain't like him. Anyhow, I finally figured out that he might be that kid, so I thought I better come down and see."

Lessman looked doubtful. "He never mentioned having any kin around here."

Wolverton studied his hat. "Well, I don't suppose he knew where I was. I don't write too good, and I can't never think of anything to put in a letter."

"You don't write your family at all?"

"Well, I kept intending to. Did this

142

winter. I been homesteaded up there most of five years now, and I did get a letter written and told her where I get my mail and such. Anyway, she wrote back right away. That's when I found out Levi had died. I wasn't real keen on her marryin' him, but he sure did treat her good."

"Had you known him before?"

"Naw, nobody did. He rode into Fort Robinson asking if anyone knowed about this ranch he was wantin' to buy. I guess I figured he was probably runnin' from somethin', and sooner or later it'd catch up with him and she'd be left a widow."

"Well, I guess she was."

"Yeah, but not like I figured. Funny, I never thought of nothin' like pneumonia killin' him. Anyhow, she said Wayne was workin' for you, and then she stopped gettin' any letters, and just the money each month, so she thought maybe somethin' was wrong."

Lessman thought about it for a minute. "Well, I guess you got a right to know. How much you want to tell his ma is up to you. I ain't wrote to her, 'cause it sure ain't my place to tell her nothin'."

He related the whole story to Wolverton, starting with hiring Wayne at the train station in Waltman, ending with Pete's warning and Wayne's subsequent flight.

"We ain't heard nothin' atall from him since. If I got him sized-up right he's still around, and I don't believe for a minute he's any sheep stealer, but we kinda get to wonderin' sometimes. There's sure a lot of stories goin' around."

Wolverton nodded. "I've heard a bunch. If half of them was true the kid's Jesse James, Wild Bill, and Wyatt Earp all rolled into one. Who'd they catch with the hides?"

"Guy by the name of Vance Gurley."

Wolverton snorted. "If Vance told me it was rainin' out I wouldn't unroll my slicker till I checked. He couldn't tell the whole truth if he had to."

"You know him then."

"I know him. He's got sort of a homestead a ways down Willow Crick from me. If he ever made an honest dollar I missed it."

LaDonna could contain herself no longer. Since Wolverton had begun she had felt an increasing buoyancy come over her. Hearing all the things Wayne had said verified whisked away all her growing doubts like dandelion seeds in a gust of wind.

Her face a study of mingled joy and fear she blurted out, "Do you know where he is? Do you know where he'd go or where he's hiding? Can't you find and tell him we know he's innocent?"

Surprised, Wolverton looked at her. "Well! Sounds like he might be just a little special!"

LaDonna turned crimson. "No! Well, yes. Well, I just don't want to see him running and running if he didn't do anything wrong."

She sat back down, torn between

embarrassment and her desire to ask a hundred questions. Wolverton was speaking again. "You don't have any idea where he went?"

"Not a one. Don't have any reason to think he's still in the country, other'n not thinkin' he would leave until he's settled this."

Wolverton turned his hat around several times in his hands, studying it. "Well, I guess that's what I need to know. I'll do some nosin' around and see what I can turn up at Fox's place. My homestead is about four miles from his place, and I know most of his steady hands."

"He's got a lot of new hands too, I hear."

"He does that. Pretty tough customers. We figure Fox is gettin' set to run us homesteaders off Willow Crick, but sounds like he might be after your government range too. You mind if I sleep in the bunkhouse tonight?"

"Stay and welcome. If you know Vance Gurley maybe you can get

146

somethin' out of him."

There was an edge in Wolverton's voice as he replied, "I thought I might just have a talk with Vance."

He walked from the room. As the door shut behind him LaDonna sprang from her chair again. "Dad, you've got to do something! Wayne could be hurt or killed or almost anything and we don't even know where he is and he probably thinks we hate him and that we believe all the things everybody has been saying about him and — " Lessman held up both hands. "Whoa, whoa. Don't get all lathered up! There isn't a thing we can do till we find out where he is. He's a big boy. He can take care of himself."

That night LaDonna lay awake far into the night. She remembered the time she had turned her ankle — almost accidentally — on a stone as they walked across the yard. He had caught her to keep her from falling. She remembered the feel of his arms, the rock hardness of his strength. She ached to feel those arms, to hear the quiet resonance of his voice, to be able to say something that would bring that furious flush running to his face. She sighed as she pictured him in her mind, then caught her breath as an unwanted picture of him, hurt and hunted, intruded. When she finally fell asleep she slept fitfully, her mind besieged by alternating dreams of joy and disaster.

She was up at sunrise, and saw Wolverton ride out of the yard. She went downstairs and found her mother had already prepared breakfast and her father was eating. She wondered why they were stirring so early, but said nothing. She sat down at the table, and her mother put a plate of breakfast in front of her.

As they finished eating, Lessman said, "Why don't you pack a few things and we'll go into Casper for a couple of days? Your mother has some things she wants to get, and I want to talk to the sheriff."

She looked at him sharply. "The sheriff? Why?"

He picked his teeth for a minute before answering. "Well, according to what Wolverton said last night, this Vance Gurley is the one that was caught with our hides. He claimed the kid was splitting with him. The sheriff had a warrant swore out for the kid, but Wolverton says nothin' atall was done to Gurley."

LaDonna looked back and forth between her parents. "That doesn't make any sense! Why would they swear out a warrant for one and let the other go scot free?"

Lessman nodded. "Another thing — Wolverton says there ain't nothin' the law can do about either one unless I file some kind of complaint. There ain't no law against sellin' my sheep if I don't care. I never filed no complaint on the kid, so how come they tried to arrest him?"

LaDonna felt like an idiot. She knew that! Part of the studies her mother insisted she continue dealt with practical matters of law. Her father's words had triggered her memory, and she could almost read the words from the text in her mind.

"Oh, Dad, that's right!" she exclaimed. "I don't know why I didn't think of it! Fox couldn't file a complaint for theft of your sheep! The sheriff should know that. Then there isn't anything against Wayne at all, is there?"

Her dad replied seriously, but with a twinkle in his eyes. "Well, I guess there is, but there might not be if you'd get some things packed so's we can go to town."

LaDonna fled upstairs, grabbed her valise, and began packing. She wanted to sing, to dance, to shout. She couldn't wait to get to town and clear the whole thing up, then tell Wayne and . . . She stopped in mid-motion, a dress across her arm. Tell Wayne! How could she tell him? She didn't even know where he was! Thoughtfully she finished packing and took her valise downstairs. She put it into the Model 'T', then crossed to the bunkhouse.

She stepped to the front of the bunkhouse and knocked on the door. From inside someone yelled, "Who is it?"

"LaDonna. Is Pete in there?"

The sound of boots crossed the floor and the door opened. Pete stepped out. "*Si*, Señorita LaDonna. What is it?"

"Pete, do you know where Wayne is hiding?"

"Señorita LaDonna, I have not see him since the day the sheriff come," he evaded.

"That's not what I asked, Pete," she insisted. "Do you know where he's hiding? Could you find him?"

Pete continued to evade the question. "Why, Señorita? Why should you wish for me to find him?"

LaDonna realized she was going to learn nothing Pete didn't want her to know. She said, "If you think you could find him, would you? I need for him to know that we know he didn't

151

steal our sheep. The charges against him are just trumped up, and we're going into Casper to get them cleared up. Will you see if you can find him and tell him?"

Pete studied her for several moments before answering. "I try, but I do not know if I can find him. I know two, three places where maybe he might hide for winter. Maybe I find him. I find him, I tell him for you."

"Thank you, Pete. Oh, thank you!" She grabbed Pete's arm and squeezed it, then turned and ran back to the car. She settled down into the seat and wrapped the blankets around her. She was smiling as the car bounced out of the yard.

8

THE Model 'T' made slow progress. The snow had mostly thawed from the south slopes, but climbing out of every draw on the north slope was difficult and treacherous. Lessman sat ramrod-straight, gripping the steering-wheel with both hands, sawing it back and forth constantly as he fought ruts, rocks, and snow. Just north of Dry Creek where he and Wayne had been ambushed he turned the car around to back up a hill the car wouldn't pull in low gear. The rock-strewn hillside bumped and bounced them as they struggled half-way up the hill. Then they could not find enough traction to go farther. Lessman set the brake and got out.

He removed a coil of rope from behind the seat and walked to the top of the hill. Tying one end of it securely to the base of a cedar, he brought the other end back to the car. He looped it around the rear axle, then through the spokes of the wheel, and tied it. Putting the car back into gear he let the wheel spin slowly until the rope wrapped around the axle and tightened. As the wheel continued to turn, the axle served as a winch, and the car began to crawl up the hill. When they were close to the cedar the rope was anchored to, he stopped. The surface of the hillside was gravelly enough at this point to give them the needed traction, so he set the brake and disconnected the rope.

He had just recoiled the rope and returned it to the car when a voice stopped him. "That's a real cute trick, Lessman. Shame you didn't keep your eyes open while you was doin' it."

Lessman whirled to face three men on horseback. His back stiffened and the muscles on his jaw bunched as he recognized the speaker. "Fox! What are you doing on my place?"

Fox grinned as he got down from his horse. The two men with him had both removed their right gloves and sat with their hands resting on their thighs, inches from their gun butts. They moved their horses away from each other, until they sat about ten feet to either side of their boss.

Fox walked over to the car. "Mornin' Mrs. Lessman. LaDonna. Now ain't you about the prettiest little filly a man ever seen! Sure galls me to see a girl as pretty as you havin' to live with all them stinkin' sheep-herders."

Lessman's face flushed a deep red. His eyes widened and his hand shook as he pointed a finger at Fox. "Fox, you got somethin' to say you say it to me, and then you get off my place. What do you want?"

Fox ignored him and turned to his men. "You know what, fellas? We was wondering what the best way was to get them stinking sheep out of this country — I think we just found it. What say we let this pretty little thing enjoy our company for a while instead of Lessman's?"

LaDonna and her mother let out simultaneous gasps of disbelief as Lessman lunged for the thirty-thirty carbine standing against the front seat. He grabbed it and turned just in time to catch the barrel of Fox's pistol across the side of his head. He crumpled into the snow without a sound, and Fox picked up the rifle, tossing it to one of his men.

He was still grinning as he turned to LaDonna. "Now, sweetie, you wouldn't want me to have to kill your old man, would you? You just climb out of that contraption and climb up here with me. We're going to take a little ride together."

LaDonna stared back and forth from Fox to her mother. All she could say was, "Mother!"

Marion Lessman's voice was surprisingly controlled. "Mr. Fox, just what is it you intend to gain by kidnapping my daughter?"

Fox never stopped grinning. "Why that's simple Mrs. Lessman. I figure that's the one thing that'll get that bull-headed husband of yours persuaded to get rid of them sheep. Anything else, he'll fight, but he ain't going to take no chances with his little girl, now, is he? When he comes to, you tell him we got his girl and he ain't gettin' her back till every last one of them sheep is sold and shipped out of this country."

His grin had faded by the time he finished his little speech, and the wicked gleam in his eyes had given way to a fevered fire. He turned back to LaDonna and snapped in a brittle voice, "Now get outa there and come on."

LaDonna's chin lifted and her eyes flashed as she retorted, "I'd rather die than go anyplace with you!"

Marion held up a hand. Her voice retained its calm and she spoke to LaDonna but watched Fox. "I think it's OK, LaDonna. If you don't go, he will kill your father. I don't think he's crazy enough to harm you — in any way. He knows if he lays a hand on you, anybody in this country will hang him on sight."

She continued to stare steadily at Fox. "As a matter of fact, that will probably happen anyway if you do this. You can't possibly think you can kidnap a girl and still stay in this country!"

Fox growled, "You let me worry about that. You got thirty days to get rid of them sheep. For that long, your girl will just be visiting over at my place. After that I ain't responsible for what happens to her."

He reached out and grabbed LaDonna by the wrist, pulling her out and shoving her toward his horse. He lifted her into the saddle, then swung up behind her. Marion watched helplessly as they rode from sight.

When they had gone, she began rubbing Lessman's face with snow, holding one handful of snow against the growing lump above his left ear.

It was nearly thirty minutes before he began to come around. He opened his eyes slowly, and gazed without comprehension at his wife for nearly half a minute before memory rushed back into his eyes. "LaDonna!" he croaked.

Marion held him still. "She's gone. Fox took her, but I don't think he'll hurt her. Bill, he's just gone crazy! He thinks he can use her to force us to sell off all the sheep."

Lessman looked at her, eyes still dull but troubled. "He said that?"

"Yes. He said he would keep her at his place for thirty days, and if we haven't gotten rid of all our sheep he wouldn't be responsible for her any more. I think he meant he would turn her over to his men! Bill, he wouldn't really, would he? I mean, Fox's men aren't that bad, are they?"

Lessman sat up, holding his head with both hands. "I don't know. Not his old hands, but I don't know about hardcases like those two with him. I don't even know if he still has any of his good hands."

Marion breathed, "What will we do?"

Lessman gripped the car to steady himself as he fought to stand. "Well, we sure ain't gonna wait no thirty days to see what he'll do. Let's get back home and get the boys. We'll just ride over to Fox's and get LaDonna back."

Marion shook her head. "You can't ride that far with that knot on your head."

He got into the car and leaned his head against the steering-wheel for a minute before answering. "I've survived worse. It'll clear up by the time we get back to the house. Get in. We'll get home easier than we came. The south slopes are uphill this direction, and the snow's gone from them."

They manoeuvred the car back toward the ranch, Lessman alternating between periods of clarity and dizziness. During the dizzy times he would wipe a hand across his eyes and Marion would grab the steering-wheel to keep the car in the general vicinity of the road. They bounced over the rocks at a much greater speed then either safety or the condition of Lessman's head warranted.

As they sped into the yard the hands appeared from everywhere, alarmed by their unexpected return. Lessman stepped from the car and leaned against it to steady himself. He began to bark orders. "Curt, get the men saddled up. Saddle the big roan for me. Fox and two of his gunhands have kidnapped LaDonna. He said they were taking her to his place. We're going after her."

Curt stood motionless, staring from one to the other in shocked disbelief. "Kidnapped LaDonna? What for?"

Lessman shrugged, "Gone plumb crazy, I guess. Says we either sell off all our sheep or he'll turn her over to his men."

Curt continued to stand in confused refusal to accept what he heard. "Aw,

I can't believe that! There ain't no cowpoke in this country that crazy for a woman. If they was, they'd just quit and head for Casper. They can buy all the women they can handle on the Sand Bar. They wouldn't bother LaDonna none!"

Lessman gritted, "Curt, stop arguing and get them horses saddled. Fox has gone crazy and them new hands of his are bad apples if I ever seen any. I ain't leaving LaDonna there to find out how bad they are. Now move!"

He shoved away from the car and started unsteadily for the house. Marion followed him, calling out to the foreman, "Curt, saddle my sorrel. I'm going too."

When they came out of the house some thirty minutes later, dressed for a long cold ride, and each carrying a bedroll and rifle, Lessman walked steadier. They tied the bedrolls behind their saddles, holstered the rifles in the saddle scabbards, and swung aboard. They looked at the assembled crew as Curt rode up on a big line-back buckskin.

Curt reported, "I left old Hial to feed as best he can while we're gone. They won't get fat, but they'll live."

Lessman nodded and rode out, Marion riding beside him. Curt dropped in behind, with Scotty beside him, followed by Morgan and Curly. Suddenly Lessman stopped and turned around. "Where's Pete?" he demanded.

Curt frowned, "Bill, I don't know. He saddled up and packed his bedroll while you was gone. I think it was somethin' LaDonna told him just before you left. Then you came back when he was just ready to leave. He listened, then rode out fast. He didn't say nothin' to me at all."

Lessman pondered it for a minute, then wordlessly turned and started north again, riding hunched over in the saddle, free hand gripping the saddle-horn much of the time. It soon became apparent that Marion was leading the way, and Lessman's horse was simply keeping pace.

They rode steadily the rest of the day. The sun was nearly gone when they topped a long hill and looked down at the head of Buffalo Creek, and saw the buildings of the Paul Gantz ranch spread below them.

Marion turned to the man. "It's less than an hour to dark. We'd just as well stop over here for the night and get an early start in the morning. If we rode straight on, it would be after midnight when we could get to Fox's place, and it would be foolish to ride in there in the dark."

Without waiting for an answer she turned and led the small cavalcade down the trail and into the yard. They were met in front of the house by the huge bulk of Paul Gantz.

"Well, if it ain't the Lessmans!" he boomed. "Get down and come in. What brings you out this way? If you wasn't along, Marion, I'd say that outfit of yours was fixin' to hang somebody. Bill, you look plum pale

164

around the gills! What's up?"

Marion stepped down and reached a hand to steady Lessman as he dismounted. He reached to shake hands with Gantz and said, "Paul, Fox hit me over the head and kidnapped my girl. Said he was takin' her over to his place. We're goin' after her."

Paul's mouth opened and shut several times as he looked back and forth from Bill to Marion. "Whaaat?" he finally rumbled. He turned toward Lessman's crew. "You men take care of your horses and go on down to the bunkhouse and make yourselves at home. Bill, you and Marion come on in the house. Tell me what happened. Kidnapped your girl! Dotty! Come on out here. We got company. Fox kidnapped your girl!"

"Marion!" The voice from the porch emanated from what must have been the biggest woman in Wyoming. Dotty Gantz stood six feet two inches in her stocking feet and would have weighed at least three hundred pounds. Her rosy cheeks were flushed as though she had been standing over a hot stove, and the laugh wrinkles at the corners of her eyes attested to a disposition as bright as her husband's. She crossed the porch and stepped into the yard with surprising agility and caught Marion in a quick hug that nearly made her disappear.

She stepped back and held Marion at arm's length. "Marion, what's this I hear? LaDonna kidnapped? My land, what on earth can that man be thinking of? Oh, you must be worried sick! Come inside. We'll have Cookie put on some supper for you and your men, and you can tell us about it."

They went inside, Paul and Dotty Gantz both talking excitedly, asking questions, and Paul saying repeatedly, "Kidnapped your girl! We'll ride over there with you in the morning. All of us will. Kidnapped your girl! Why the whole country will back you on this, Bill. Never heard of such a thing. Not in this country. Ain't no question but a man's gotta be hung for something

166

like that. Kidnapped your girl!"

The darkness was just beginning to fade the next morning as the Lessmans and Paul Gantz walked out of the house. The four hands of Lessman's had been joined by three grim-faced cowboys from the Gantz ranch, raising their number to ten. Eight of the men wore pistols, and all had rifles, including Marion. Lessman looked a great deal better this morning. His eyes were clear, his walk steady, and his voice was firm as he mounted up and turned to the men.

"One thing, men," he announced. "I don't want anybody shot if we can help it. Most of Fox's men are good men. They won't stand for what Fox has done. Don't nobody start shooting unless you have to, and don't let it get out of hand. I want LaDonna back, and I want Fox. That's all."

Without waiting for an answer he wheeled his horse and rode out with Marion beside him. Paul Gantz and Curt rode side by side next, then the

167

rest of the combined crew followed. Dotty Gantz stood on the porch, hands in her apron, and watched them out of sight.

Their pace slowed toward midday as the melting snow and warming ground made the footing slippery and uncertain. It was past noon when they rode down the hogback into the hollow across the ridge from the Fox ranch. They pulled up and Lessman talked quietly. "Curt, you take our men around north and cross the crick. Spread out and come in behind the ranch yard from the east."

Without a word Curt nodded and rode away with the Lessman crew following. Lessman turned to Gantz's foreman. "Jack, you do the same from the north, but stay on this side of the crick. Try to figure out where all our men are, so we don't shoot toward each other if it comes to shootin', but just stay put."

Jack nodded and rode off with his men, and Lessman turned to Marion and Paul Gantz. "We'll wait half an hour, then we'll cross over to the south road and ride into the yard from the south. If we're lucky, maybe we can get this done with no shootin'."

The three dismounted to rest while they waited. There was very little talk, each wrapped in his own thoughts. They all knew that the country would never be the same, no matter what happened here today. A respected rancher had let a feud with his neighbour destroy his mind, and he had committed an act this country would neither forgive nor forget. Fox would surely be hung, shot, or run out of the country. The fabric of the land had been torn, and however it was mended the scars would remain forever.

When the half-hour had passed, Lessman stood from under the tree against which he had been leaning and said, "It's time. Let's go get her."

They mounted up without a word and rode west, then south, to intersect the south road out of sight of the ranch buildings. As they topped the rise above the slope leading down to the road they stopped and looked the country over carefully. There was no movement in sight. Warily they rode down the road and turned north toward the ranch.

As they approached the yard they could see nothing out of the ordinary. Not many horses were in the corral, but that was normal. Most of the hands would be out doing the day's work. Nobody showed in the yard.

As they entered the yard a hand carrying a bucket of water saw them and stopped. He turned to shout something to the bunkhouse, then saw Morgan standing beside a tree not twenty feet from him, rifle held loosely but pointed at his chest. Morgan said softly, "I wouldn't say nothin'. Just stand real easy where you're at."

The man swallowed nervously. "Who are you? What do you want?"

Morgan said, "Relax. You'll find out pretty quick."

Marion, Lessman, and Gantz fanned out facing the house, rifles held loosely across their saddles in front of them. Lessman called out, "Hello the house!"

There was no response for fully two minutes, then a voice called out from the bunkhouse door. "Fox ain't to home. He ain't been here for two or three days. China the cook's the only one in the house."

The three turned to face him. "My name's Bill Lessman. I run the Rockin' R. You foreman here?"

"Nope. Not no more. Was till this mornin', but I just got my walkin' papers."

"Who's foreman now?"

A voice from the corner of the house replied, "I am."

They whirled to face the new voice, each cursing himself for carelessness. The man standing at the corner of the house was about five feet ten inches tall, average build, with striped California wool pants and a silk shirt. He wore two guns, tied down, and stood with his thumbs hooked in his gunbelt inches in front of each gun. "You folks lookin' fer someone?"

Lessman responded, "I'm lookin' for Fox. He hit me on the head yesterday and kidnapped my girl. I want her, and I want Fox."

The gunman let out a short laugh. "You think you can ride in here with some cock-and-bull story like that and ride out again? Mister, you got more guts than brains."

The hand from the bunkhouse interrupted. "Wait a minute! You say Fox kidnapped your girl?"

Lessman replied without taking his eyes from the gunman. "He did. Him and two gunmen with him. I aim to either kill him or take him to Casper to be tried and hung."

"Get outa this, Cramer," the gunman barked. "You ain't foreman and you don't work here no more. You three get off them horses and get in the house. You ain't leavin' till the boss gets back."

Lessman started to lift his rifle when the gunman's hands streaked to his gun. They were already clear of their holsters when three rifles barked as one and the gunman was knocked backwards. He made one effort to rise up on an elbow, then fell back and lay still. The combined crews of Lessman and Gantz stepped from their concealment, three of them with wisps of smoke drifting from their rifle barrels. Silence hung like a cloak across the yard.

The silence was shattered by another rifle shot, coming from the hill above the yard. A man dropped a rifle and tilted out from the hay mow door in the top of the barn, falling to the ground. The voice of Ray Wolverton carried into the yard. "That one was about to do some back-shootin'. He won't now."

Wolverton rode into the yard, rifle still held across his saddle. "Saw you folks ride by this morning, so I thought I'd tag along and lend a hand. You found the kid yet?"

Lessman shook his head. "Fox kidnapped my girl. We're looking for her."

He turned to the hand the dead gunman had called Cramer. "How come you got your walkin' papers?"

Cramer looked bitterly at the figure of the dead gunman. "'Cause I run a cattle ranch, not a hang-out for outlaws and gunmen. I wouldn't have nothin' to do with his tryin' to run your herders off the mountain and such, so he canned me."

"Looks like you just got your job back," Lessman observed. "Where can we find Fox?"

Cramer wrinkled his forehead. "I ain't got any idea. If he done what you say, he'll be tryin' to hide out someplace. Only places I can think of are a couple line shacks over south, and an old trapper's cabin in the mountains. I'll sure be glad to ride with you to check them out."

Lessman looked around. "Any other

"hands on the place?"

"Couple in the bunkhouse. One just rode back in this morning."

Lessman turned to Curt. "Go invite 'em out here, Curt. Let's talk to them."

Two of the others went with Curt and disappeared into the bunkhouse. They returned a of couple minutes later, herding a couple obviously reluctant men. At the sight of one of the men Lessman stiffened and Marion let out a gasp. "That's one of them!" she cried. "That's one of the men that took LaDonna!"

The man looked like he was about to run, but ten rifles staring at him changed his mind. He began to stammer. "It wasn't my idea! I didn't have no idea what he was gonna do. I swear it! I wouldn't'ta touched her neither."

Lessman cut him short. "Where is she?"

"I don't know! Honest to God, I don't! Montana, he rode out and met us and they sent me back here to make sure nobody left here lookin' for 'em, but I don't know where they went. Honest, I don't."

Gantz's foreman stepped forward, holding a coiled rope. "Tie his hands, Curly," he said as he tossed the rope to Curly.

Curly tied his hands behind him quickly and tightly. He looked questioningly at Lessman, then at Gantz. Lessman turned to Curt. "Take Mrs. Lessman into the house, Curt. Check for any indication of where they might be."

Curt placed a hand on the reluctant elbow of Marion Lessman and steered her toward the house. As they passed out of hearing she heard her husband say, "If you want to change your mind, it just might save your life."

She and Curt checked through the house without finding anything but accumulated filth. As they returned to the porch she looked up and gasped. Hanging from a limb of a tree in the yard, the body of the gunman turned slowly back and forth. The men were leading their horses into the centre of the yard, and Lessman approached them.

"We checked out all the buildings and everything," he told her. "I think Cramer's telling the truth. They haven't been here."

She studied his clenched jaw and pale face. "But where else would they be?"

"I don't have any idea. There's those there shacks some of the men can check out. We'll ride back to the Gantz ranch till we hear."

"And if they don't find her? What then?"

"I don't know, Marion. I don't know."

The rode out, faces set grimly, hearts aching within them. Their minds felt as hopeless and helpless as the image of the gunman twisting slowly at the end of the rope. It seemed like it was a part of themselves they left dangling there — a part of themselves that had died.

9

WAYNE and Charlie had pulled their traps. Their catch had been dwindling the past couple of weeks, and Charlie had begun to be concerned that they were trapping that section of the creek down too far. They stood in the doorway of the hide shack, surveying the results of a winter's work.

Charlie nodded his head once emphatically. "Yessir, that's not a bad year's work."

Wayne asked, "What do you think they're worth?"

"Must be pertnear six or seven hundred dollars' worth, I'd say. Soon's the ground firms up . . . "

The conversation was interrupted by a nicker from Charlie's horse, and an answering nicker from a horse out of sight among the trees. Wayne picked up his thirty-thirty and watched to see who was coming. Pete rode out of the trees into the clearing.

Wayne grinned and called, "Pete! How'd you find me?"

Grinning broadly Pete stepped down and shook hands. "It is good to see you, Keed."

"How'd you find me?" Wayne asked again.

"Curt, he hire herder last fall that ride down from Kaycee," Pete explained. "He say he see new cabin at head of Crazy Woman Creek, like maybe trapper. I think, direction you leave camp, maybe it be where you winter. I take chance and come here. Ride all day, all night, all morning. I am ver' glad I guess right!"

Wayne shook his head. "I sure thought I'd be harder'n that to find! Pete, this is Charlie Taylor. He's an old friend of my dad's."

Charlie extended a hand. "Pete, I'm plumb glad to meet you. Wayne's told me some about you. But I don't reckon you rode up here to say 'hi'. Come in and have a bite of dinner and tell us what brought you."

Pete's grin faded, "*Si*. I will eat and sleep and let my horse rest, and then we must go quickly. Señor Lessman, he has been hit on the head by Fox, and Fox he has steal the Señorita LaDonna."

Wayne felt the colour and heat of his body drain, beginning at the top of his head and draining down until he felt a cold chill through the emptiness of his being. "Stole LaDonna? What do you mean?"

Pete looked at him steadily. "He take her away. He and two of the gunmen he has hire. He say he keep her until Señor Lessman sell all his sheep. He say Señor Lessman not sell all his sheeps in thirty days, he give LaDonna to his men to do what they want with her."

Wayne shuddered with the chill that had iced his veins. "What's Lessman doing?"

Pete shrugged. "He is getting his men together when I leave. They will ride to Fox's place to find her, but I think they will not find her there."

"And if they don't, then what?"

"I do not know. I do not think they know too. Señor Fox, he has gone loco in the head now, I think. His men, they are ver' bad. I think the *señorita* she is ver' much in trouble with them."

Wayne looked across the tops of the mountains that separated him from wherever LaDonna might be. The muscles along the line of his jaw knotted, and his hands clenched and opened helplessly. Twice he opened his mouth to speak, then shut it again. Finally he croaked, "Let's eat," and wheeled into the cabin.

Pete and Charlie followed him into the cabin. Pete collapsed into a chair and Wayne and Charlie went about setting food on the table. As they ate they discussed LaDonna's situation.

Charlie said, "We got to figure Fox don't aim for her to get hurt none

— not right away nohow. That means he'll need to have someplace to keep her where he can keep her away from them men o' his without riskin' her gettin' away."

Wayne chimed in, "If they plan to keep her long, they'll need someplace they can get supplies without arousing suspicion."

"But where nobody's apt to look or see her," Charlie responded.

Pete nodded. "*Si*. I think of that. It have to be place where people live. If it is a place ver' alone, people will see them going there with the supplies. I think maybe I have the idea. Keed, the brother of your mother come to see Señor Lessman . . . "

Wayne jerked upright. "What? You mean Uncle Ray? Is he here?"

Pete held up his hand. "*Si*. He has heard from your mother that you do not write. She tell him where you work, so he ride to our ranch to find out."

Wayne leaned back in his chair. "Well, whatdya know! I knew he was somewhere in Wyoming with a homestead or something, but didn't have any idea where. Whatdya know!"

Pete went on. "He is saying the man who say he is together with you in the stealing of Señor Lessman's sheep, he is a man who has the homestead close to him. I am thinking that if he is saying this for Señor Fox, and if Señor Fox is not having him arrested, it is maybe that he is together with Señor Fox."

"That makes sense," Charlie agreed.

Pete concluded, "So I am thinking maybe that would be the good place to look for Señorita LaDonna."

"You know this guy's name?" Charlie asked.

"*Si*. It is Vance Gurley."

"Never heard of him. You know where his place is?"

"*Si*. Señor Wolverton say it is where Willow Creek and Buffalo Creek run together."

"I know the spot," Charlie stated. "Real hard-scrabble homestead there. Junky place."

They discussed the lie of the land around the homestead from Charlie's memory. He had the western man's ability to remember details of the land, even in places he had seen only in passing, and they made tentative plans. They allowed Pete and his horse to rest, and rode out before daylight the next morning.

They rode all day and into the night across the mountains, continuing always south and west. They stopped a couple hours at dark until the moon rose. By its light they passed the outline of the bald top of Roughluck Hill, reaching nearly seven thousand feet, then swung west again. When they finally stopped it was Charlie who spoke.

"I reckon we'd just as well hold up here now. We can't be more'n a mile or so east of Buffalo Crick. Just afore daylight we'll cross over and work up on top. We'll come in above Gurley's place from the north."

They loosened the cinches of their

saddles, moved the bits from the horses' mouths so they could graze, and rolled into their bedrolls, exhausted. No one slept.

They dozed lightly between small talk until the greying of the eastern sky heralded the coming of daylight. Rising silently they packed up, tightened the saddles, and rode on. They kept to the sides of the draws, now, staying low enough to remain unseen, but keeping from the deep snow in the bottoms.

Dropping down to Buffalo Creek they crossed and climbed the hills on its west side, then turned back south. The sun was not yet in sight, but it was fully light when Charlie silently signalled them off their horses.

They tied the horses in a small clump of cedars where they wouldn't be easily seen, and walked in a crouch to the top of the hill. As they approached the crest they dropped to all fours and worked their way to clumps of sage brush from which they could survey the area below without being seen.

Charlie had led them unerringly to the hill overlooking Gurley's homestead. It was everything he had said it was. The house was not built of logs, nor of any consistent material. It appeared to have been built of materials scavenged from old buildings, ruins, and scrap piles.

The roof had shingles in places and tin in others. There was no door. In its place was what looked like an old buffalo hide nailed at the top and hanging loose. The windows were made of brown paper soaked in oil, rather than glass. A crooked piece of stove pipe jutted through a corner of the roof, held upright by wires tied to the roof. The entire house looked like it wanted only the excuse of one gust of wind to collapse.

The corral bore the same appearance. It was made of cedar posts with the small branches only partially clipped off. They were stood against each other and lashed together with pieces of twine, wire, and old cloth, making a more-or-less solid wall of posts. Every ten feet or so a post was set in the ground to give the fence stability. The tops of the posts were whatever length the cedar had grown, so the corral varied in height from four feet in places to ten feet tall in others. Daylight showed between the irregularities of the posts. That, combined with the uneven top, made it appear impossibly ragged.

"See them horses?" Charlie whispered.

"Yeah," Wayne responded in kind. "All four branded FX."

"I think you guessed right, Pete."

"Smoke from the chimney. Somebody's gettin' the fire lit."

"Let's slip down there."

Darting from clump to clump of the sage brush they worked their way down the slope. They came into the yard at the back side of the corral and moved to the corner nearest the house. Charlie motioned Pete around the house one direction and Wayne the other, indicating that he would approach in the middle, going directly to the front door.

Wayne's stomach was knotted and his mouth dry. He could feel the blood pounding in his ears. He wiped a hand across his mouth. He drew his pistol, checked its loads, and replaced it in its holster for the fifth time. He levered the action of his rifle quietly, far enough to see the brass of the cartridge in the chamber, then closed it just as quietly. He looked across the openness of the yard in the direction Charlie had nodded, and stepped away from the corral.

He watched Pete dart in a half-circle to disappear behind the house as he walked into the open. His boots made no sound on the frozen mud of the yard. He stepped around a small ridge of snow to avoid the crunching sound that would alert anyone listening of his approach. When he had gone far enough to see the window on the far side of the house he began walking directly toward it, watching Charlie approach the door directly across the yard.

He was about fifteen feet from the side of the house, and Charlie was about twenty feet from the door, when a voice from the corral stopped them cold.

"That'll be far enough! Drop them rifles!"

Wayne froze in his tracks, turning his head to look. Directly behind Charlie, where they had just come through the gate from the corral, stood two of Fox's gunmen, each with a pistol in his hand. Wayne cursed himself for not thinking to check the corral. He and Charlie both reached their hands slowly away from their bodies and let their rifles fall to the frozen ground.

The two gunmen stepped on out into the yard, each leading a saddled horse. The shorter one grinned. "Well now, we was just fixin' to ride a circle to see if you boys was around. Looks like you saved us the trouble!"

The other gunman yelled toward the house. "Fox! We got company!"

The buffalo hide covering the door

swung aside and Fox stepped out, blinking at the brighter light. He swore. "Where'd they come from?"

The taller gunman answered. "How should I know? Want us to get rid of 'em?"

Wayne's mind was racing. Fox wasn't wearing a gun. Both he and Charlie still had their pistols, but the gunmen had the drop on them. To draw and shoot might be possible, but would almost certainly mean the gunmen would shoot at the same time. To try to lunge sideways as they drew would only slow their own draw and invite certain death. He looked at Fox. Fox kept looking back and forth from Charlie to Wayne. His eyes burned with an unnatural fire. He kept licking his lips and opening his mouth as though about to say something, but never saying anything. He walked a slow half-circle around the two, toward his two gunmen.

Fox was almost around to his two men when there was a sudden burst of sound from the house, followed by a shot, then two more shots in rapid succession. As the gunmen's eyes jerked toward the house, Charlie and Wayne acted in perfect unison. Faster than the eye could respond their hands flashed to guns that seemed almost to leap from their holsters, belching fire. Dust leaped from the gunmen's shirt fronts and they staggered backward, a look of incredulous surprise on both faces. One of them fell backward and the other folded, falling forward. They both lay without moving.

Some part of Wayne's mind registered five more shots, evenly spaced, from a single gun, coming from inside the house.

At the instant the shooting started, Fox made a lunge for one of the gunmen's horses and leaped into the saddle. Leaning forward across the saddle-horn he dug his spurs into the animal's side and yelled. The horse left the yard at a dead run. Wayne struggled to get moved where he could shoot around Charlie, but was unable to do so before Fox was out of pistol range, running the horse flat out. Charlie stood with his gun ready, watching for signs of life from either of the gunmen, then he moved to pick up their guns.

Wayne sprinted to the house and ducked past the buffalo-hide door, gun in hand. Gurley was sitting against the near wall with his hands lying limp on the floor, palms turned upward. His head leaned back against the wall and his eyes were open, but unseeing. Pete stood outside the remains of the rear window, its oiled paper hanging crookedly from one corner where Pete's gun barrel had swatted it in. LaDonna stood beside the window, holding Gurley's pistol at arm's length at her side, staring at the dead homesteader.

Wayne's heart lurched as he saw her. Her hair was dishevelled and loose. Her face was smudged with black on one cheek and she had a large bruise across the side of her face. She lifted her eyes slowly until they met Wayne's, and she gave a strangled little cry that was choked off in the middle. The gun fell from her fingers as she raised her arms toward Wayne with another choked sob. He stepped to her and wrapped his arms around her, holding her against himself as her bottled emotions began to fight their way to the surface.

She clung tightly to Wayne as the first sob, sounding more like a hiccup than a sob, jerked from within — a sob that never broke through her tightly compressed lips. A second followed it, and a third, growing increasingly close together until the tide of bottled sobs broke through in a wordless wail. The floodgate of her emotions broke then, and she cried, saying something over and over that Wayne couldn't understand.

He held her until the tide of terror had spent itself, tears running down his own face, not even aware that he was saying, over and over, "It's OK honey. It's OK now."

Wayne held her that way, the arm that was around her still holding his gun, his other hand stroking her hair as her face lay buried in his shoulder, until she quieted. She drew back, wiping her cheeks with the back of her hand, saying, "I — I — I'm sorry. Oh, I'm so glad to see you."

He holstered his gun just as she collapsed into his arms again. She sobbed for another minute before again drawing back. He held her with a hand on each of her arms, just below her shoulders, and looked into her eyes. "Are you — did they — uh, have they — ?"

She sobbed, "No. No. No, it's OK. They didn't hurt me — or anything. They were going to, and they kept arguing about it, and making all kinds of horrible jokes about who got me first, and Fox wouldn't let them have me till Dad got rid of his sheep and then he said he didn't care what they did with me and I didn't think anyone could find us and they smelled so awful and I couldn't get away and I didn't know where you were and this place is so terrible and they made me cook their meals and they ate like a bunch of hogs and Fox kept staring at me with that horrible gleam in his eyes and they kept touching me when he wasn't looking and I was afraid to go to sleep at night and oooooooh . . . "

Wayne pulled her to himself again and pushed her face back against his shoulder to still the torrent of words. He kept saying, "OK, it's OK, it's OK," because he couldn't think of anything else to say.

When she had regained control she pulled away and walked to the washstand. She dried her face with a towel, then turned back to Wayne.

"I shot him! I shot Gurley! Pete broke the window out and shot at him and missed. Then Gurley pulled his gun out and Pete shot again at almost the same time he shot. Gurley missed but Pete hit him and he dropped his gun. I grabbed it and I shot him. Wayne, I stood there and shot him and shot him and shot him until it was out of bullets and I couldn't stop. I just kept squeezing the trigger over and over. Please take me outside!"

Wayne put his arm around her and led her past the buffalo hide into the bright light of the yard. The two gunmen lay where they had fallen. The remaining horse stood nervously, snorting occasionally at the smell of blood. Wayne noticed idly the spatters of blood across the horse's rump, and reasoned it must have come from a bullet passing through one of the gunmen.

Charlie spoke. "Kid, Fox got away. We better figure out what we're going to do next. He may ride clean outa the country, but crazy as he looks I'm doubtin' it."

Wayne was having trouble even thinking about Fox. His eyes were filled with LaDonna. He reached out to touch the bruise on her face. He asked, "Who did that?"

"Gurley. I was pouring their coffee and he ran a hand up under my dress, and I poured the coffee on him. He got up and yelled and hit me. I think he would have killed me if Fox hadn't stopped him."

Charlie interrupted. "Kid, we gotta get movin' one way or another. Maybe you best take the girl home and me'n Pete'll try to follow Fox."

Wayne looked at him, listening for the first time. "No. Fox is mine. I can track him."

Pete walked over to the gunman's horse, speaking softly. He picked up the trailing reins and stroked the horse along the neck, rubbed beneath the bridle around the ears, and steadied him down. Mounting, he rode out of the yard.

Half an hour later Pete rode back into the yard, leading the three horses they had left tied in the cedars. Wayne and Charlie were still arguing about

197

what Fox was most likely to do and who should ride after him, but it was obvious that Charlie realized he wasn't going to change Wayne's mind.

"I still don't like it, Kid," he said, "but if that's the way you want it, it's your party. Me'n Pete'll take the girl home. You just be danged awful careful, and remember everything I taught you."

Wayne nodded grimly as he watched them mount up. He started to help LaDonna into the saddle, then blushed and turned away at the flash of leg exposed as she swung into the saddle. Flustered, he gave a little half-wave as they started out of the yard, then LaDonna stopped and turned her horse.

She sat there looking at him for a long moment, then said softly, "Wayne, be careful! I want you to come home."

Wayne tried to answer but couldn't get any words past the lump in his throat, so he just nodded and turned to his own horse.

He rode out, following the obvious trail left by Fox's fleeing mount. He did not see LaDonna sitting in the yard, motionless, watching him until he was out of sight.

10

WAYNE rode at a fast trot, easily following Fox's trail. Because the running horse that Fox was riding threw up chunks of snow and frozen mud as he ran, he could pick out the trail two hundred yards ahead, and follow it without conscious thought. His conscious mind was busy studying the country, watching for places where a hunted man might turn around to stage an ambush. He kept watching his horse's ears, aware that he would hear or smell another horse or another man far quicker than he himself would.

He continued on the trail all morning. As midday passed the ground surface grew slippery with melted snow and mud on top of still frozen ground. The trail showed increasing signs of time, and he knew he was getting farther and farther behind Fox. He also knew that Fox must slow his horse or ride him to death, and he resisted the urge to hurry his own mount.

By mid-afternoon the trail grew harder to follow as Fox slowed his horse, but he continued to leave plenty of tracks because of the warmth of the sun. The melted mud stuck to the horse's hooves and left a trail of small pieces of mud across the rocky and frozen places. Close-up, sometimes, the trail was difficult to see, but looking ahead Wayne could pick out the line of it leading always south-east.

By the time the sun dropped behind the Wind River Mountains to the west, Wayne could tell he was gaining ground. The trail was noticeably fresher, but also noticeably more difficult to follow. Fox was beginning to think about hiding his trail, and that, combined with the growing darkness, would make further tracking tonight impossible.

He began to look for a campsite to

stop for the night, and soon spotted a place ideal for his purpose. A small spring trickled from the rocks at the edge of a draw, making an area of unseasonably early grass for about thirty yards. About a hundred yards farther, against the same side of the draw, a fallen tree left a small space between itself and a high, overhanging bank. The spot was far enough from where his horse would be hobbled that someone stumbling onto the horse wouldn't be right on top of where he was camped, and it offered excellent cover from all sides.

Unsaddling his horse he hobbled him out on the good grass, then made a small smokeless fire on which he made a pot of coffee. He drank three cups of the coffee with some dried biscuits and jerky, then turned into his bedroll. He went to sleep listening to the night sounds his ears were so accustomed to hearing.

Once during the night he heard his horse snort. Alert and silent, he lay with his gun in hand. In a few minutes he heard the soft tearing sound of the horse biting off grass, eating again, so he went back to sleep.

He woke in the hour before dawn and again lay still and listened. When he was satisfied nothing was amiss, he got up. He held each boot upside down and shook it vigorously, then put them on. He had never found any visitors in his boots of a morning, but he knew others who had, so he always checked.

He again made coffee over a small fire, ate two biscuits with another piece of jerky, saddled his horse, and rode out.

He rode this morning with his rifle held across the saddle in front of him. He let the horse pick its own pace, concentrating on watching every piece of brush and cover. Fox must surely know he would be followed, and he would choose his time and place to stop and watch his back-trail.

The trail turned up a narrow canyon

and Wayne stopped. If he followed that gash in the earth he would be helpless against an ambush. The trail led up the north side of the canyon, just high enough to avoid the snow that still filled the bottom. The chance of the canyon leading any place was slim. Most such canyons reached back into the mountains, growing narrower and deeper as they went. Almost without exception there would be a place within a mile that was impassable. There always was. The water from snow melt or sudden rains would follow these canyons, periodically washing out a softer section of ground. That created a waterfall, sometimes fifty feet high or more. When the water was gone, that left a sheer bank across the canyon, flanked by the sides too steep to climb. A man on foot might climb around the obstacle and continue, but a man on horseback had no choice but to turn back.

That meant Fox was looking for a place to camp for the night, or he was setting up an ambush, or else he planned to climb out of the canyon before its sides grew too steep to do so. Deciding which he was doing would mean the difference between life and death for Wayne, or perhaps between following the trail and losing it completely. But how could he decide what a crazy man was thinking?

Wayne dismounted and walked slowly across the canyon mouth. It was about two hundred yards across at this point, and he crossed slowly, studying the ground. Nearly to the other side he found what he was seeking. The frozen ground at the edge of a small depression was marked by a fresh skid mark. A horse's hoof had come down on the uneven surface and slid about three inches. Following up the canyon from that mark he found another about twenty feet away. Beyond it he saw a small spot of dry grass lying flatter than the surrounding grass.

Fox had returned this way! He had ridden up the canyon last night, leaving tracks. Then he had ridden back this way this morning on frozen ground, riding carefully to hide his trail. That meant he had camped somewhere up the canyon, and was already on the move again.

Wayne turned back toward the mouth of the canyon, following on foot the direction the trail led. Quite a ways farther he found another scuff mark, then a broken twig on a small clump of sage, then the impression of half a horse's hoof in the edge of a patch of snow. Calculating the direction Fox had taken, he muttered, "Well, he's still headin' south."

He turned back to his horse and mounted, following the faint indications of Fox's trail. He rode with extra caution now, the skin on the back of his neck tingling every time he approached anything that could hide an ambush. He knew he was no more than a couple hours behind his prey.

The country around him grew familiar. He was in country where he had herded his band of sheep, and just being in familiar surroundings helped him relax. The trail led out of the stand of timber it had been going through, toward a rocky outcropping that marked the edge of a long slope.

The sun was warm on his face. An eagle soared silently in a lazy circle of the sky. The creak of his saddle and the jingle of the bit chain seemed like soft music of spring. In spite of his mission, Wayne felt like singing.

The spell was broken by a sudden explosion of light, and his world turned suddenly black. He felt himself leaving his horse and landing hard on the frozen ground as he swirled into the endless depths of oblivion. He never even heard the report of the rifle, barking from the rocks ahead.

The first hint of consciousness was pain. He slowly became aware of a roaring ache that seemed to be pushing his head into the ground. He opened his eyes and saw only a murky haze, moving in a slow circle. His stomach churned, and he closed his eyes and lay still, lacking either the will or the ability to move.

He couldn't remember where he was. He couldn't remember what he was doing. Silently he muttered in his mind, "Horse musta throwed me."

He tried to turn over on his side, and cried out sharply at the unexpected stab of pain the movement brought to his head. He reached a hand to it and felt a sticky wetness. He held his hand in front of his face and squinted at it. A blur of red swam in front of his eyes. He stared at it stupidly, trying to understand.

Slowly his mind began to function. He remembered Charlie saying something. 'You be danged awful careful . . . '

The words echoed in his mind like distant sounds only half heard. 'Danged awful careful . . . what I taught you . . . careful . . . taught you.'

He shook his head to clear it, and cried out again at the pain and dizziness that movement caused. He lay back down on the ground. Lying with his eyes closed his memory re-enacted the fight at Gurley's homestead. He watched in his mind as the two gunmen fell to the ground and he turned to the house. He saw the buffalo-hide door and past it the room's interior. He saw LaDonna standing with the gun hanging in her hand.

'LaDonna!'

The memory of where he was, and why, flooded back upon him. His eyes flew wide open and his head swivelled back and forth, looking wildly around. He exclaimed, "I've been shot!"

He saw his horse standing about fifty feet away, reins dragging the ground. He looked toward the jumble of rocks from which the shot must have come, but saw no movement. He looked for the position of the sun and was startled to realize it was mid-afternoon. "I musta laid here two or three hours," he mumbled.

His rifle lay where it had fallen, almost within reach. He said to himself,

"He got me. He laid for me, and got me. He musta seen me fall and thought I was dead. Well, we'll just have to see about that."

He struggled to his hands and knees and crawled to a battered and crooked cedar tree. Using it for support he hauled himself to his feet. He gripped it hard till the waves of dizziness and nausea passed.

He pushed away from the tree, took two steps and fell. The mountainside swirled in a circle around him, then slowed. He fought his way back to his hands and knees and stayed there for thirty seconds, then slowly straightened his body until he was upright on both knees. When he had rested another minute, he shifted to one foot and staggered back to his feet. He stood there swaying for fully two minutes before the world came back into focus.

He took a short step and stopped, waiting for his body's reaction. Then he tried a second, and a third.

He picked up his hat and rifle after

three attempts, then lurched unsteadily toward his horse. It eyed him warily, not liking the smell of blood or his master's erratic actions, but it was trained to stand when the reins were dropped. He tossed his head and rolled his eyes, stamping a front foot from time to time, but he stood his ground.

"That's a good old pony, Streak. Stand easy. Eeeeesy. Just stand where you're at."

He kept crooning as he staggered closer. When he was within reach, he bent slowly to pick up the trailing ends of the reins, then stood as the waves of dizziness again passed. "Streak, I'll just give you a whole gallon of oats for that. Not all at once, though. You're too good a horse to founder."

He put his rifle in the scabbard, fed the far rein up across the horse's neck, and dragged himself painfully into the saddle. When he had sat there for several minutes he took off his neckerchief and wrapped it around his still bleeding head. Then he eased his hat as far as he could down over it, grimacing at the waves of pain it caused, using the hat to hold the crude bandage and stop the bleeding.

When he had sat a few more minutes he spoke to the horse again. "OK, Streak. I guess the world's done bein' dizzy for a little bit. Let's go find that bushwhackin' idiot."

He was worried, even through his pain. If Fox had lost his sanity as completely as it appeared, he was capable of anything. Since the ranch was the focus of his obsession, they were in danger. He felt a driving urgency to be there, to know what was happening, to protect them. To protect LaDonna. He dug his heels into the horse's side and he picked up the pace of his walk.

He was in the draw just north of the Lessman ranch when he heard the shots. He pulled up to listen. He couldn't tell where they were coming from, except that they were all in the area of the ranch yard. He dismounted

212

and started to walk up the hill, but his dizziness overcame him, and he sat down abruptly.

When the weakness and dizziness had passed, he stayed on his hands and knees and moved to the base of a clump of sage. Lying on his stomach he worked painfully forward until he could see the entire Lessman ranch laid out below him.

In the centre of the yard a man's body was stretched motionless. Two horses lay dead in the corral. The collie dog that was the Lessman family pet was dead at the corner of the porch. At the corner of the barn another man was propped against the side of the building with one leg angled out in an unnatural direction, obviously broken. He was holding a rifle, but making no attempt to use it.

While he watched he detected three shots coming from the house, and at least two rifles shooting from windows of the bunkhouse. Their fire was being returned from a clump of boulders at the rim of the low cliff overlooking the yard. When Wayne picked up the puffs of smoke from the rifle in the boulders he put the picture together rapidly.

Shooting from the cover of those boulders, someone had opened fire on the ranch yard, evidently killing at least one man and wounding another before the rest gained cover. The residents of the ranch were now pinned down. The area around all the buildings was within range of the rifleman on the cliff, and they could not move from the cover of the buildings without coming under fire.

From below, their return fire was largely ineffective against the unseen assailant in the rocks. His only real danger was a chance ricochet, and firing from below most of those would glance harmlessly into the air, rather than back down into the sniper's shelter. When the occupants of the ranch had gained cover, the assailant had apparently begun to shoot any living thing that appeared in the yard.

When he had sized up the situation, Wayne slid backward out of the brush and backed down the hill. When he was below where he could be seen he stood carefully and returned to his horse. "Come on, Streak," he instructed the animal. "Let's see if we can circle around and give Fox a little company."

It had never occurred to him that the rifleman might be anyone other than Fox. He felt certain that Fox's frustration and obsessive hatred had compelled him to wait from his vantage-point for the object of that hatred. He had evidently snapped completely, lost all reason, and begun to kill anything that moved.

He rode back down the draw to a point well below the Lessman ranch, where it came out into the valley in which the ranch was nestled. Crossing that valley he ascended the range of hills south of it, then turned back west, riding just below the crest of the ridge. When he was even with the sound of the sporadic firing, he again dismounted. Holding his rifle in one hand, he crawled on hands and knees to the crest of the ridge and looked over.

Less than fifty yards in front of him he could see the cluster of boulders that housed Fox. Fox's horse was standing about two hundred yards off, to the east, trying to graze with the bridle bit still in his mouth. As Wayne crawled into sight the horse's head came up sharply, but there was no indication Fox had noticed.

Watching the cluster of boulders, Wayne stood up. His surging adrenalin pushed back the wave of dizziness, and his legs felt less trembly and uncertain. Cautiously he approached the boulders.

The rifle in the boulders fired twice while he was walking slowly toward it. Then, when he was about fifteen yards away, he came into clear view of the assailant. It was Fox. He was lying on the ground with his rifle rested in a niche between two rocks. From his vantage-point he had a clear view of the entire ranch yard, but nothing of him was visible except the part of his head above the sights of the rifle. From below he was an impossible target.

"Drop the gun, Fox!"

Wayne held his rifle at his hip, finger on the trigger, pointed at the centre of Fox's back. Fox stiffened and turned his head slowly to look across his shoulder. When he saw Wayne his face blanched.

"You!" he rasped. "I shot you! You're dead!"

"Not quite. Now stand up and drop the gun."

With a snarl Fox rolled to the side and whipped his gun around. It spouted fire and lead even as it was swinging to bear on Wayne. Wayne's rifle roared an answer, and Fox flopped back against the rocks. Both men levered new shells into the chambers of their rifles, but Wayne's rifle barked again before Fox could bring his to bear. His body bucked again, but he continued to lift his rifle. Wayne levered another shell into the chamber and fired again, then again before Fox finally began to release his grip on his own gun.

As Fox's rifle fell from his fingers it landed on the rocks and discharged, the bullet careening harmlessly into space. He tried twice to say something and failed. Then as Wayne watched, the fierce and frenzied gleam in his eyes faded and went out, and he lay there staring into nothing from wide and unseeing eyes.

The adrenalin washed out of Wayne and his suddenly weak knees would no longer hold him. He staggered to a large boulder and sat down where he could still watch Fox's body. "You got to be dead," he told the unseeing corpse, "but there ain't no way I'm turning my back on you anyway."

When he felt his strength would allow it, he got up again and stood still for a minute. Heaving a big sigh, he walked over and picked up Fox's rifle. As he straightened with it the dizziness came again, and he fought it off before backing away, still watching Fox's body warily.

He put his own rifle in his saddle scabbard and held Fox's rifle across his saddle as he turned and rode back the way he had come. When he came to the road he turned to follow it to the ranch. The little black specks were floating aimlessly in front of his eyes again as he rode slowly into the yard. He heard someone yell for him to get under cover, but he simply couldn't muster the strength to respond. He rode to the front porch of the house. As he dismounted, Lessman yelled from the door. "Get under cover, Kid! Fox is up on the cliff shootin' everything that moves."

Wayne's own voice sounded to him like something far away, and it echoed in his head like someone talking in a barrel as he answered: "I got him. I went around and got him. Here's his rifle."

Then the world went black.

He couldn't figure out where he was. At first he thought he was in his sheep wagon, but the light was wrong. Then he realized he was looking at curtains screening sunlight through a window. His hand moved against the softness of a sheet.

'A sheet!' he thought. 'I'm in a bed.'

As he moved a sharp pain stabbed through his head. With the pain, awareness flooded back, driving away the edges of fog in his mind.

'I made it,' he told himself. 'I got Fox, and I made it clear home.'

As he thought the word 'home' he gave a mental start. 'Home? When did this get to be home? Oh well, it's a nice thought.'

He folded the covers back and sat up. As he did the bed-springs groaned in protest. A chair scraped in the next room and an instant later Lessman's form appeared in the doorway.

"Well, you woke up! We was beginnin' to think you was goin' to sleep all week!"

Wayne was confused. "How long have I been asleep?"

"Oh, just since day before yesterday evenin'," Lessman grinned.

"Am I OK?"

"Yeah, you'll live. Doc says you lost a lot of blood, and you got a furrow in your head deep enough to plant corn in, but you're in pretty good shape, considerin'."

Wayne felt the bandage on his head gingerly as Lessman continued: "You feel up to gettin' up for a bite to eat?"

Wayne was suddenly ravenously hungry. "Yeah. That sounds good."

"Your clothes are there on the chair. LaDonna washed and ironed 'em for you. She's been kinda anxious to talk to you too."

He stood there for a few more minutes as though he was fishing for words that didn't come easy. Finally he cleared his throat and said, "Uh, I been sendin' your ma that half o' your wages all along. We never did believe you was no thief. You shoulda stuck around. I, well, I want you to know we're just plumb awful grateful for you gettin' LaDonna back for us. We was near outa our minds and just couldn't find her nowheres."

Wayne interrupted him. "It was Pete and Charlie that figured out where they had her. Are they here?"

"Pete is. Charlie said he had to get back and get them furs down to Kaycee before they wasn't fit to sell. He took an extra horse and said he'd be back with your share of the money for 'em."

"He was a friend of my father's."

"That's what he told us."

"Do I still have my job?"

"Why, you'd better believe you do! We never figured you'd quit. We'd sure like you to stay on permanent."

Wayne let the words soak in, savouring them as though they fed a hunger greater than his screaming appetite. Looking past Lessman he saw LaDonna looking at him from the other room, and he said, "That sure sounds awful good to me."

And watching LaDonna, it sure did seem like a good idea.

THE END

TOP HAND
Wade Everett

The Broken T was big. But no ranch is big enough to let a man hide from himself.

GUN WOLVES OF LOBO BASIN
Lee Floren

The Feud was a blood debt. When Smoke Talbot found the outlaws who gunned down his folks he aimed to nail their hide to the barn door.

SHOTGUN SHARKEY
Marshall Grover

The westbound coach carrying the indomitable Larry and Stretch headed for a shooting showdown.

FIGHTING RAMROD
Charles N. Heckelmann

Most men would have cut their losses, but Frazer counted the bullets in his guns and said he'd soak the range in blood before he'd give up another inch of what was his.

LONE GUN
Eric Allen

Smoke Blackbird had been away too long. The Lequires had seized the Blackbird farm, forcing the Indians and settlers off, and no one seemed willing to fight! He had to fight alone.

THE THIRD RIDER
Barry Cord

Mel Rawlins wasn't going to let anything stand in his way. His father was murdered, his two brothers gone. Now Mel rode for vengeance.

ARIZONA DRIFTERS
W. C. Tuttle

When drifting Dutton and Lonnie Steelman decide to become partners they find that they have a common enemy in the formidable Thurston brothers.

TOMBSTONE
Matt Braun

Wells Fargo paid Luke Starbuck to outgun the silver-thieving stagecoach gang at Tombstone. Before long Luke can see the only thing bearing fruit in this eldorado will be the gallows tree.

HIGH BORDER RIDERS
Lee Floren

Buckshot McKee and Tortilla Joe cut the trail of a border tough who was running Mexican beef into Texas. They stopped the smuggler in his tracks.

BRETT RANDALL, GAMBLER
E. B. Mann

Larry Day had the choice of running away from the law or of assuming a dead man's place. No matter what he decided he was bound to end up dead.

THE GUNSHARP
William R. Cox

The Eggerleys weren't very smart. They trained their sights on Will Carney and Arizona's biggest blood bath began.

THE DEPUTY OF SAN RIANO
Lawrence A. Keating and
Al. P. Nelson

When a man fell dead from his horse, Ed Grant was spotted riding away from the scene. The deputy sheriff rode out after him and came up against everything from gunfire to dynamite.

FARGO: MASSACRE RIVER
John Benteen

The ambushers up ahead had now blocked the road. Fargo's convoy was a jumble, a perfect target for the insurgents' weapons!

SUNDANCE: DEATH IN THE LAVA
John Benteen

The Modoc's captured the wagon train and its cargo of gold. But now the halfbreed they called Sundance was going after it . . .

HARSH RECKONING
Phil Ketchum

Five years of keeping himself alive in a brutal prison had made Brand tough and careless about who he gunned down . . .

FARGO: PANAMA GOLD
John Benteen

With foreign money behind him, Buckner was going to destroy the Panama Canal before it could be completed. Fargo's job was to stop Buckner.

FARGO:
THE SHARPSHOOTERS
John Benteen

The Canfield clan, thirty strong were raising hell in Texas. Fargo was tough enough to hold his own against the whole clan.

PISTOL LAW
Paul Evan Lehman

Lance Jones came back to Mustang for just one thing — revenge! Revenge on the people who had him thrown in jail.

HELL RIDERS
Steve Mensing

Wade Walker's kid brother, Duane, was locked up in the Silver City jail facing a rope at dawn. Wade was a ruthless outlaw, but he was smart, and he had vowed to have his brother out of jail before morning!

DESERT OF THE DAMNED
Nelson Nye

The law was after him for the murder of a marshal — a murder he didn't commit. Breen was after him for revenge — and Breen wouldn't stop at anything . . . blackmail, a frameup . . . or murder.

DAY OF THE COMANCHEROS
Steven C. Lawrence

Their very name struck terror into men's hearts — the Comancheros, a savage army of cutthroats who swept across Texas, leaving behind a bloodstained trail of robbery and murder.

SUNDANCE: SILENT ENEMY
John Benteen

A lone crazed Cheyenne was on a personal war path. They needed to pit one man against one crazed Indian. That man was Sundance.

LASSITER
Jack Slade

Lassiter wasn't the kind of man to listen to reason. Cross him once and he'll hold a grudge for years to come — if he let you live that long.

LAST STAGE TO GOMORRAH
Barry Cord

Jeff Carter, tough ex-riverboat gambler, now had himself a horse ranch that kept him free from gunfights and card games. Until Sturvesant of Wells Fargo showed up.

McALLISTER
ON THE
COMANCHE CROSSING
Matt Chisholm

The Comanche, McAllister owes them a life — and the trail is soaked with the blood of the men who had tried to outrun them before.

QUICK-TRIGGER COUNTRY
Clem Colt

Turkey Red hooked up with Curly Bill Graham's outlaw crew. But wholesale murder was out of Turk's line, so when range war flared he bucked the whole border gang alone . . .

CAMPAIGNING
Jim Miller

Ambushed on the Santa Fe trail, Sean Callahan is saved by two Indian strangers. But there'll be more lead and arrows flying before the band join Kit Carson against the Comanches.

GUNSLINGER'S RANGE
Jackson Cole

Three escaped convicts are out for revenge. They won't rest until they put a bullet through the head of the dirty snake who locked them behind bars.

RUSTLER'S TRAIL
Lee Floren

Jim Carlin knew he would have to stand up and fight because he had staked his claim right in the middle of Big Ike Outland's best grass.

THE TRUTH ABOUT SNAKE RIDGE
Marshall Grover

The troubleshooters came to San Cristobal to help the needy. For Larry and Stretch the turmoil began with a brawl and then an ambush.

WOLF DOG RANGE
Lee Floren

Will Ardery would stop at nothing, unless something stopped him first — like a bullet from Pete Manly's gun.

DEVIL'S DINERO
Marshall Grover

Plagued by remorse, a rich old reprobate hired the Texas Trouble-shooters to deliver a fortune in greenbacks to each of his victims.

GUNS OF FURY
Ernest Haycox

Dane Starr, alias Dan Smith, wanted to close the door on his past and hang up his guns, but people wouldn't let him.